TRIOLET

TRIOLET

Indifference

•

The Hero

•

Music and Senescence

Dipanjan Rai Chaudhuri

NIYOGI BOOKS

Published by

NIYOGI BOOKS

D-78, Okhla Industrial Area, Phase-I
New Delhi-110 020, INDIA

Tel: 91-11-26816301, 49327000
Fax: 91-11-26810483, 26813830

email: niyogibooks@gmail.com
website: www.niyogibooks.com

Editor: Jyoti Kumari
Cover Design: Global Publishing Solutions
Design: Shashi Bhushan/Niyogi Books

ISBN: 978-93-81523-05-6
Publication: 2012

Other than actual historical persons and events, portrayed according to the author's interpretation, all characters appearing in this book are a work of the author's imagination. Any resemblance to actual persons is entirely coincidental.

Printed at: Niyogi Offset Pvt. Ltd., New Delhi, India

CONTENT

INDIFFERENCE

8:00 AM TO 12 NOON

I had been preoccupied the previous night when I walked from the bus stop to the house where I was a lodger, otherwise I would have noted his arrival earlier. Whether that would have prevented the precipitation of the crisis which occurred in my personal life, or merely saved it for another day, I cannot tell. At the time I was convinced of the former possibility, but I am far from sure now.

Returning from a walk with my girlfriend, I had indeed a lot to be preoccupied about.

Both of us hailed from a sleepy market town, eight hours from the metropolis by a combined journey of slow train, ramshackle bus and van-rickshaw, this last being a contraption for transporting vegetables and humans, consisting of a platform on wheels pushed by bicycle pedals.

We did not know each other, however, before we met at the college for undergraduates where, unwittingly, both of us had enrolled ourselves. It was natural for us to drift together, two pieces of flotsam on the metropolitan waters. Also, we were studying the same subject,

English literature. Our town, as it happened, had two excellent, though segregated, schools for boys and girls, set up by old landlords and endowed by their émigré descendants, one of whom took pains to attend managing committee meetings, where he insisted on and was able to enforce and cajole the maintenance of a high standard in the teaching of English.

She was pretty. It cannot be that she was unaware of it, but, perhaps, small town admiration was not valued by her sufficiently to give her enough self-confidence to carry herself with the usual aplomb of pretty girls. This, coupled with small town shyness, made her less noticed than might have been expected. In fact, as I learnt later, the girls of her class considered her arrogant. Now, my aura of rusticity was unmistakable and faded very slowly, and she had me placed quite accurately. That she noticed me at all was the doing of George Bernard Shaw. A Shaw play was taught by the only impressive teacher in the department, a Shaw enthusiast like my old English master at school, who had practically made a potion of GBS to be forcibly fed to unfortunates like me in whom he had seen 'a glimmer, though no more, of interest'. Smelling a compatriot, however unenthused, the teacher at the college started bouncing ideas off me in class, which led to a certain notoriety.

She approached me in the quadrangle one afternoon for help with Shaw. A little conversation confirmed her suspicions regarding my origin, though she was a little less surprised than me to learn just how much we had in common. Hugely reassured, both of us started talking like long lost friends.

I saw him when I was going to buy razor blades from the corner shop. It was a bright morning and the shadows were sharply defined. He was lying on the sidewalk outside a pathological laboratory. His beard and hair were unkempt and matted, and dirt caked his hands and feet. He wore a shirt, blackened with grime and in tatters, and a loincloth through which came out and rested on the stones of the walk a huge, oval growth, his scrotum, distended till red veins stood ready to burst on its surface, glistening evilly in the morning light. His eyes were open. It was a Sunday and there was a small crowd of market-goers near his head. A small man, the owner of the local hair-dressing shop, two chairs and mirrors in a sliver of space between two mansions, was holding forth on the iniquity of the municipal corporation which allowed such sights to linger in a public place as they 'outraged the modesty of women'. Crows sat hopefully in groups on overhead telephone cables and electricity poles, and pi dogs came sniffing only to be shooed away by the people joining and leaving the fluid little confabulation around the man. Most of the men had early morning bleariness around the eyes with a day's stubble on the face and plastic bags in their hands from which erupted vegetable stems and a smell of stale fish.

She lived in a girls' hostel, which strictly limited male access to an anteroom presided over by a formidable chaperone, perennially huddled over the telephone, which she relinquished only reluctantly to her wards, reserving the right to follow the conversation from this end. Apart from the door there was only a skylight high up and the gloom and squalor were compounded by the weak light from a lone electric bulb, naked without shade or cover. You had only to sit beside an inmate for the matron to start a string of warnings and threats. She was convinced that all male visitors, whatever the relationship declared in the visitors' register, had designs on the virtue of her girls. She invariably knew when someone had filched time for herself between the end of classes and her return to the hostel, and was resentful of Sundays when everyone was free to receive calls and visit the home of the accredited local guardian, no questions asked. My own boarding house was scarcely more conducive to the germination of romance, peopled as it was by my bawdy contemporaries and flaunting the same concern for the protection of our virtue via a notice in chaste vernacular: No ladies beyond this point.

So, when I picked up the courage to ask for her company without a Shavian excuse, it had to be a Sunday at some place away from our dwelling houses. According to freshman folklore, the walled parks and gardens, bordering the green expanse in the heart of the metropolis, were safe from the intervention of neighbourhood toughs and policemen. On our third outing, I remember, we were crossing the green when the wind rose, dust swirled and swept past us and, finally, the rain came, fat drops hitting us on the face and drenching our clothes in no time. Laughing, we ran to the shelter of the nearest tree, and there I held her hand. After a moment's hesitation, her hand curled around mine. It was the closest we came to a declaration of love. The earth moved for me. I learnt later, during a sharp exchange of words, in fact, that though the earth did not move for her, she too had been deeply affected. For both of us, it was the first serious contact with the opposite sex, quite different from the chance meeting of eyes at marriage parties.

There followed a very happy interlude. We roamed about the metropolis, walking the broad avenues, bordering the green, as well as narrow streets going deep into densely packed tenement houses with people overflowing onto the sidewalks and beyond, until the ebb and flow of the pulse of the city and its patterns of sleep and siesta became second nature to us. We talked of our childhoods and schooldays, our parents and families. Did we talk of aspirations? We weren't ambitious, all we wanted at that time was to make good in the indifferent and unhelpful world of the metropolis. Our greatest fear was to return to our birthplace as failures.

I came out again to take delivery of laundered clothes from the 'steam laundry' as it called itself on the signboard above a door set at the top of a flight of steps. My everyday clothes went to the washerman, who came twice a week to collect all our soiled linen in a huge bundle which he balanced on the back of a donkey and took away to be washed in one of the several ponds of the locality. Actually I was indulging in a luxury, because we were to go to a film show that afternoon. It was an adaptation of Shaw's *Pygmalion*, and called itself by the same name. This dates my narrative to a period before the sweeping success of the musical super hit *My Fair Lady*, based on the same play. No theatre ever showed *Pygmalion* after *My Fair Lady* hit the world, though the immortals must have weathered successive bursts of Shavian invective once the picture of Higgins folding Eliza in fond embrace reached the eternal abode.

Somebody had thrown a sack over the lower portion of the man's body and this had drastically reduced his visual appeal to the voyeur. The flies, however, knew what was underneath the sacking. But now only the occasional passer-by would stand for some time and hover hesitantly over him. His eyes were open and he was staring at the sky, which was reflected with disconcerting clarity in each eye, the dazzling whiteness of cloud formations standing out against the darkness of the pupils. For minutes on end he wouldn't blink and then, all of a sudden, the shutters would come down. Just when you would start to think that perhaps he had dropped off, the eyes would again open. But the only place he looked at was the sky. Not a word passed his lips. I had seen people bending over him and asking him his name and whereabouts without the slightest response from him. His gaze remained unwavering, skywards.

I suddenly felt a twinge of responsibility. The boy at the sweetmeat shop gave me a paper cup which I filled with water from a roadside tap and brought to his mouth. Imagining, perhaps, a parting of the lips, carefully I decanted a little water onto his mouth. The water just dropped off. Only a few tiny drops remained lodged in the cracks of his parched lips, where they glistened like minute jewels. Guiltily,

I remembered a kettle on the boil and hastened away, pinning my hopes on the pathological laboratory which would open its doors any moment now. Persistent unpleasant vibes from my private life soon crowded him out of my awareness.

As she gained confidence, her natural joie de vivre began to assert itself. Her face was now full of vivacity and her movements gained a certain elegance. Never unintelligent, she could sensibly keep up her end of any conversation. She started to cut all but the most interesting classes and was often seen at the coffee place, sparkling in the middle of a large group of young men and women sitting around two tables joined together. Her high spirits converted her pretty looks to almost a thing of beauty. Suddenly she was showered with male attention, a fact she brought home to me forcefully one day, though whether the situation was engendered intentionally or through unconcern I never gathered enough courage to find out.

Of course, I saw her strolling in the quadrangle or enjoying herself in the coffee place in male company, and I was not so besotted a fool that I wouldn't be able to link this up with her inability to give me time, but I continued to believe that her relationship with me was special, telling myself that I shouldn't be so possessive as to grudge her the time she gave her friends and should, in fact, be pleased at her popularity.

She suffered from a chronic throat condition which had recently worsened, a part of my mind told me, because of constant chattering. I fixed an appointment with a doctor, who was also the son of a family friend. He had rooms at a busy crossing and I waited for her on the kerb, idly watching the evening wash of the homeward urban tide, trying, it was a game I played with myself, to attach a story to every interesting face which passed.

I saw her on the opposite side of the road and, as the memories of other occasions when she had met me at a roadside rendezvous rose to cloud my eyes, I forgot the current strain in our friendship, and started crossing the road, almost calling out her name, when I saw that she wasn't looking for me and her face was turned towards a companion. He was a year senior to us and distinguished by the, then rare, possession of a motor-bike and the inevitable nickname of Killer, arising from the diversity in the female occupants of the pillion seat. By the time I had taken all this in, they had found me. He looked quizzically at me and told her, 'So, I'll be back after an hour'. She said nothing at all to me and simply followed me to the doctor's chambers. The fee had to be deposited in advance, and she firmly turned down my offer to pay. That was all the conversation we had, she browsed through a glossy magazine till her turn came. I took her in, the doctor looked at her throat and wrote a prescription, which included rest to the vocal chords, made some desultory small talk with me, and the evening was over. There was a quarter of an hour still to wile away and she waited patiently at the kerb. So palpable was her disinterest in her surroundings that I didn't suggest sitting at a tea shop as would have been the easy thing to do. I know I should have left but I had yet to shed all my country feathers, and I tortured myself till the Killer arrived, this time on his bike. She clambered aboard and they left without noticing my presence as it were.

I couldn't, after that, go on deluding myself regarding the state of the relationship, although at least once every day the thought would cross my head that she was bound to realise the shallowness of her present existence and come back to me. The morning was the worst part of the day. I realised how apt was the description of people waking up with a heavy heart. There was actually this heaviness in my chest and, half-awake, my first query, every morning, was 'Why am I feeling like this?' It would make me wide eyed in no time, and all the recent happenings would fill my mind with remarks, pictures and notions which made concentration and the follow-up of rational and logical train of thought difficult. Teachers were conducting furious tutorials in hastily requisitioned alcoves as the preparation holidays before the university examinations drew near, but I could hardly pay attention for half an hour without distracting thoughts seizing control. The same would happen when I tried to study in the evening. The only work I seemed still able to undertake almost normally was writing notes, and these I made copiously, wondering all the while how I would assimilate the resulting mounds of matter before the examinations.

We were to meet at the movie theatre at 2:30 pm, and I started early because I wanted to pick up a book from a classmate whose house fell on the way to the theatre. From afar I could tell the man was still spread-eagled on the pavement. It was a hot noon and he was quite alone now. The scorching sun had dispersed all visitors. He hadn't stirred it seemed and the dark pupils were still fixed on the sky, whose hard metallic brightness would have dazzled any other eyes.

The laboratory was open and I entered the lobby where there was a desk marked 'ENQUIRY' in long-faded letters. The lobby was dark and cool, the desk manned by a person with whom I had a nodding acquaintance from the time he had to make repeated visits to our lodgings to draw blood for tests from a fellow boarder down with suspected malarial fever. I asked him whether they could do something for the poor soul outside. He was quite cross. He said, 'You are perhaps the tenth person to ask us this. Why, I say why? Just because we do some tests on what is happening inside you, it doesn't make us a hospital, or does it?'

I shrank from taking charge myself because I knew nothing of what the metropolis did in such cases and how one connected oneself to the relevant channels, and honestly I didn't have too much time to spare. I had the book to pick and I had also offered to buy the tickets. I thought I would make another appeal, and asked the clerk whether it was possible to meet the manager.

He flew into a rage. 'Manager, now. Nobody can do his work without having to bother his head about a street cadaver. See,' he pointed dramatically at the people awaiting their turn for tests, 'so much work is to be done and he wants the manager'. As I went on standing at his desk without replying to his diatribe but also without showing any tendency of moving away, he finally ran out of steam and, wordless with exasperation, waved a hand towards the dark innards of the laboratory. The way to the manager's office lay through the animal room, housing cages of mice, guinea pigs and rabbits, and one full-grown sheep, the complete silence enveloping so many living beings mingling eerily with the mixed smell of disinfectant and excrement.

The manager heard me out and asked me to sit. Placing his elbows on the table, with palms facing one another, index fingers touching, he looked me in the eyes and said suavely, 'Of course, we must do something.' My heart fell, because I understood immediately that the 'we' was being used as a nurse uses it with a child, meaning really 'you'. I understood that the laboratory would do nothing, nor would anyone else, and trying would just wear me out. The moment I stood up, the manager understood that I would give no further trouble, and became businesslike. He pointed to the telephone on his desk and said, 'Why don't we call a municipal ambulance?', and fishing out a notebook from a drawer, wrote a number down on a slip of paper for me. He wouldn't even phone for the ambulance, apprehensive of any involvement in the matter of even his disembodied voice. I had to do it. After two or three abortive attempts, a gruff voice answered. My involved explanation was cut short and the voice asked for the precise location where the ambulance should go, and hung up with a terse declaration in four parts, 'No car in bay now. Wait for your turn. Don't ring again. All cases are emergencies.'

12 NOON TO 2:30 PM

While waiting for the ambulance I noticed the elevation of the sun. It shone down on the man with merciless clarity and his eyes were two slits on a flushed and swollen face, almost featureless like a mask in the glare. Yet, he didn't shut his eyes fully.

I tried to shift him by the torso and could hardly budge him an inch. The doorway of the laboratory was filled with heads, staring impassively at my antics. A light crowd had again formed on the pavement in spite of the glare and heat. Spectators all. No doers. Finally, the gateman of the laboratory stepped forward sheepishly. He cradled the shoulders in his arms, just lifting them from the ground, while I pulled the legs sideways. The bloated bag between his legs trailed along the ground, the fluid inside sloshing noiselessly as I pulled. The man's muscles were toneless and he was just so much dead weight. Somehow we shifted him to the shade of a broken down cart discarded by some pedlar and disdainfully left to rot by the dust-men of the municipal authorities. It was noon and much of his body still lay in the sun, but his face was saved, at least for the time being. The touch of shade opened his eyes wide, fixed as they were as before on a sector of the sky. All this activity around him had not disturbed his gaze and he showed complete unconcern about our manoeuvres on his behalf. I went on talking softly to him whenever I was near him but he never tried to respond. In fact, wherever he was placed, he never looked away from the sky. I tried to give him some water again. Seeing my efforts fail, the short-tempered clerk made the magnanimous gesture of going inside and bringing out a feeding cup. By inserting the spout between his lips I managed to fill his mouth with water. For sometime time he lay inert and water trickled down the sides of his mouth. Then he swallowed convulsively, once, twice, that was all. I couldn't put any more water into him.

After half an hour I knew I was not picking up the book today. Would I be buying tickets for the show? Panic knotted the muscles of my stomach. Another quarter of an hour and I would have to break the bad news to her.

The ambulance made a smart U-turn and stopped at the kerb. A tall heavy-set man leaped out of the driver's cabin and took in the situation at a glance.

'Lend a hand,' he said, and brought out a stretcher. A circle of men had formed around us, and, as I could have foretold, not a soul stirred. I approached the sick man and said, in the camp language usually understood all over the vast reaches of the hinterland which sent its displaced and dispossessed to the city, in wave after wave, 'You are to go to a hospital. There they will look after you till you are well. We are going to move you now. Tell me immediately if we hurt you.' He remained untouched by my plea and continued his upward gaze. I had spoken at his ear, and the closeness allowed me to see every single, slightly fair, soft hair on his face, and brought a faint sweetish whiff of rotting flesh.

I helped the driver tie the man to the stretcher by straps provided for the purpose and load the stretcher onto the patients' chamber. I had been dithering about what to do with the heavy bag between his legs. The driver wrapped it in the sack and almost threw it into the stretcher.

Everything was done, but, still the driver stood at the door of the chamber, bending down from his great height to look pensively at the man, who had shut his eyes once his line of sight encountered the roof of the ambulance. I must finally have made some involuntary movement signifying imminent departure, for the tall man straightened up and asked me, 'Who will go with me? Where is the relative?'

'He has no one here. We found him like this on the sidewalk.'

Then, he dropped his bombshell. 'I won't take a dying man to a public hospital with no one to take charge. In any case, I am quite alone today. Even the stretcher bearers have taken a day off.'

It was 1:00 pm. With desperate pleading in my stance I looked back at the circle of onlookers. Some started to shuffle away immediately and the circle thinned, but a few strong and silent rugged types stood their ground unfazed, determined to see out the unexpected Sunday entertainment right to the end. I told the driver that I needed to make a phone call, and walked confidently into the laboratory right to the manager's office, out staring the desk clerk on the way. I am sure that the manager had been briefed about the latest developments, for he immediately pushed the phone towards me almost with an ingratiating air.

That study leave spent at our town was for me another sojourn in the clouds. Within a day or two of my return, she, too, came back from the big city. Directly on her return she visited me and set up a time-table for study. She was surprisingly normal in her behaviour and I sometimes wondered which one was the dream, the past months of rejection or the present companionship. She never alluded to events which had occurred during these months and I found, consequently, neither the temerity nor the inclination to bring up the wrongs she had inflicted on me.

We studied in the attic of my house, with a door giving on the roof and wide windows kept closed on account of the glare. She came when the morning first started to warm up, and left after dusk. My mother was, at first, worried about a young woman staying for such a long time with her precious son—she had this notion that every woman I met had designs on me (O! only if it were true)—but this young woman charmed her, and, soon, she was cooking and sending up snacks to keep up the strength of the studious pair. The afternoon, in fact, was devoted to hard study. The remnant of the morning usually spent itself in desultory but intensely interesting talk about mutually known people, mainly classmates, carefully skirting, however, the territory of her special friends. By the time evening fell, the heat of the day had quite worn us out, and we came out on the roof to see the sunset, always a splendid spectacle in summer in the laterite districts, the orange powdery soil rising in a haze to refract and scatter the light of the setting sun. I wouldn't say she was insincere or that she was playacting with me, to ensure my help in her preparation for the examination. She always did what she wanted, and, if thwarted, would change tack rather than think out oblique, serpentine manoeuvres. She just wouldn't have spent so much of her time with me if she was bored.

Privacy, as always, bred intimacy, but we were, when all was said and done, small town people in the era before virginity was a state one had to jettison as soon as possible, and kissing was the ultimate in amorous play we could imagine during courtship. Vaguely I sensed that this old-worldly reticence fell as a shadow across the capers and follies of the set she had been invited to enter. Their mores were different.

Then, again, perhaps, I was walking in the footsteps of many a greater fool, when I imagined that I could tell the sincerity behind a kiss, but her kisses convinced me that somewhere near the core of her jumbled motivation of opportunism, insecurity and weakness there remained hidden a speck of real affection for me.

We returned together and as we sped across the huge bridge into the metropolis I could sense the start of her withdrawal.

She was irritated as always when her plans had to be modified even slightly. She brushed aside my suggestion that she should buy the tickets now and I would pay for them later. She sensed I was avoiding the furnishing of a reason for my delay, though she had learnt the rule that one did not ask outright for reasons in such cases. Tersely, she said, 'If you don't finally turn up I don't want to be forced to peddle tickets. Remember, I leave the hostel at 2:30 pm'. Not for a moment did she really believe that I wouldn't turn up. Her temper was rising and she could not but let me feel the heat.

When I emerged from the laboratory the crowd had swelled and moved to the open door at the back of the ambulance for a ringside view of the dying derelict who was enjoying a last and perhaps the only luxury of his life—visiting a hospital in a vehicle ordered specially for him. I had presented them with a circus to talk about for days. I was by this time feeling thoroughly irascible myself and literally shooed them away, flailing my arms till I had enough space to shut the door. I turned the handle to lock it, came to the driver's cabin, motioned to him to open the door on his left and jumped up beside him. This was a mistake, for the seat was worn down to the springs and my buttocks were bruised black and blue, as I discovered later, by the impact. The driver, a man of few words, gave me a sign of commiseration. Swallowing the pain, I looked back at the receding crowd. My last view was that of the gatekeeper of the laboratory staring at my window with open mouth. Perhaps he could not believe the folly unfolding before his eyes.

I have asked myself again and again regarding my motivation. Why did I do this? Did my heart melt? But I know myself. I am not tender hearted. Did I have an attack of conscience? But, then, this was not the first time I had seen a sick tramp left to die alone on the busy streets of the 'megacity' as the urban development department of the government likes to call our metropolis. Was I trying to make a statement which would place on record my intuitive feeling that I was somehow different from the set of people she preferred to hang out with? Therapists would no doubt pounce on this psychological angle, but I was not convinced that my subconscious would be foolish enough to ask me to cut off my nose to spite my neighbour as my old grandmother used to say. I wouldn't say I didn't know where my folly was taking me. So, it was folly, perhaps, pure and simple, inherited, my mother would say, from my father who awoke one morning and left house without money or a change of clothes. From my mother's regular diatribes against him, delivered as if he were standing in front of her, I tried to figure out, while still quite a child, what could have been the object of his flight. But because she herself hadn't a clue to his mind, I could make nothing out on that score. I had found neither indication nor anecdote of an interest in religious or other matters involving ideas or conviction, and, all in all, had long settled in my mind with the certainty and finality of childhood that his flight was from my mother and not into something.

I was not surprised when she took up with her old friends again, after her return to the metropolis, although she had last minute preparations to complete like most of us and continued our study together. But, she would often change timings at very short notice. Especially vulnerable were evenings. However, she was having problems with her set, too. Quite a few afternoons, at the library, she pleaded a headache and put off studies. We would sit in the canteen near a window overlooking the spacious grounds of the library and she would watch silently the lengthening of the shadows and the flight of parrots as they suddenly broke cover from a clump of foliage and flew into the afternoon light, shining emeralds in motion. Time to time her eyes moistened but her self-control was great and there were no tears. To me she never said anything. I doubt whether much of the time she was aware of the presence of anybody else, so engrossed was she in her preoccupations. Then, she would suddenly come alive, and lamenting the loss of time, almost run into the hall of the library and the alcove which housed our books and papers.

And, even apart from her need of preparing for the examinations with me, there remained, as I continued to imagine, a spot of warmth for me in her cold heart. As we came out of the library one evening we were faced with a sombre sunset in crimson and purple with a dark thundercloud stealing quietly over the sky. She touched my arm and pointed to the sky. As we stepped on the road I felt a hand slip into mine for a moment.

The examinations came and went. Those tense days were good, she went to the examination hall with me and we came back together. I picked her up from her hostel each morning and dropped her back in the afternoon. One morning I woke up to find the world still dark. A thundercloud filled the sky. At breakfast, flashes of lightning and thunderclaps raged outside, prologue for a cloudburst which poured down on the city for more than an hour. I rushed to her hostel the moment the rain started to falter and we came down the road quickly and boarded a bus. Midway, water began to rise, submerging the thoroughfare. The bus slowed to snail's pace, and panic spread. We left the bus and started to wade hand-in-hand through knee-deep water.

The idea was to use a by lane to reach a higher road. We were really frightened to find that this road, too, was waterlogged. Time was flying. Suddenly we encountered a bigger and higher bus which had been diverted from some badly flooded route, and we jumped on it, reaching the hall just as the last warning bell started to ring. It took half an hour for the knot in my stomach to unwind, and, as I learnt after the paper was over, she had similar trouble. We did badly in this paper. Otherwise, our results were somewhat beyond the expectation of our teachers, and they encouraged us to do better in the second part of the examinations which would be held after another year of course-work. At the notice board where the results were displayed she caught my hand and did a little jig, only to disappear with her friends, who it seemed had all just scraped through and thought this worth celebrating.

It started to rain and traffic slowed down. I began an elaborate ritual of tying a knot in my handkerchief and untying it. The driver looked at me and rummaged in the glove compartment, which was cluttered with charms of the road, torn maps, and painkillers in their bubble packs. He handed me a red rag which I was to wave outside, this being the accepted sign for an emergency.

However, in bumper-to-bumper traffic, it was difficult to give someone the right of way even if you wanted to do so. As the ambulance crawled into the emergency bay of the hospital, the rain stopped. People started to leave the ledges and doorways under which they had been seeking shelter and soon the bay was filled with relations of patients and some others who looked suspiciously like brokers. It was 1:45 pm.

I helped the driver bring the stretcher out and down to the floor of the passage which led to the emergency ward, and, prompted by him, went to look for a general duty assistant to take charge. It took time to locate someone who was not engaged inside the emergency room or going in or coming out with stuff in hand. Finally I met this man, who was taking a cup of tea handed to him by someone who, as evidenced by his gestures, was clearly the relation of a patient. He heard me out and sized me up. He explained slowly to me as if I were a half imbecile, 'If the doctor admits patient we take him in. Until then, patient party looks after patient.'

'Could the patient be taken down from the stretcher and brought into the emergency room?' I asked after repeated prodding from the driver, who had fortified his fighting powers by slipping a sizeable wad of tobacco into his mouth.

'That is up to you. We won't touch him.' He gave a dark and meaningful look at the ambulance. 'You better keep the stretcher.'

The driver nodded to me and we held a council of war. The stretcher with its load could remain outside the emergency room till nightfall and nothing more would happen. We waited till two assistants came out with a trolley and told us gruffly to clear the way. We lifted the stretcher and immediately after the trolley passed, strode smartly into the emergency room and set down our load on the floor. There were six tables, all occupied by groaning or comatose people. Two young doctors were working at two of the tables. There were other patients on the floor, which was slippery with water and body fluids of different kinds and proportions. The walls were stained and grimy. There were flies everywhere. And these were biters; you had to constantly move the bare parts of your body if you wanted to prevent yourself from being treated merely as food. Only the overhead lights were bright and strong, as if determined to illuminate every sordid detail of the inferno under them. Among the occupants of the place the new entrant we had brought in was special in his hopelessness and all shrank from him. His eyes were fixed on the tubes of light.

We were alert and the moment a table was emptied by the assistants on the advice of one of the two doctors, we swung the stretcher up on the table. It must be said that nobody remotely questioned his right of precedence. The doctor was, by this time, engaged at another table, however, and the ambulance man brought out a duty slip for me to sign. I folded my hands, but before I could make ingratiating noises, he burst out laughing, and nodded. It was 2:20 pm. I whispered 'phone' in his ears and ran out into a drizzle. He went on chewing tobacco phlegmatically. I am sure he understood my predicament and had no doubt that I would return.

She was, at first, incredulous and then incandescent with rage.

'You are so busy on a matter of life and death that you cannot attend your prior appointments? Where are you now?'

I told her. She said, 'You are quite near the theatre, in fact. Can't you make a dash for it?'

'I still don't know whether I would be free early enough to make a dash for it. I don't want to cause you further inconvenience.'

She lapsed into sarcasm. 'Oh, thank you kindly for your consideration. I had forgotten. It is a matter of life and death.' The receiver was slammed into its cradle. Was she dressed, I thought idly, had she put on make-up, confident that I would end up at her heels as on so many earlier occasions when I put off my own work to be with her, or, had she been simmering all this time apprehending a quite uncharacteristic non-compliance with her wishes? Was she so angry because it was too late for her to join her set in any of their capers, or was it for my wholly unexpected intransigence? For me it was more important to understand why I was feeling relieved, and, in fact, distinctly perky, when I should have been in the doldrums.

2:30 PM TO 5:00 PM

I had asked for a feeding cup. The assistants stared at me as if this was the first time they had heard of the item. I stared at them in reply till one of them stirred.

'There may be one in the sisters' cupboard', he muttered and, making excuses in a doctor's ear, vanished. The clock ticked on. Judging an early reappearance unlikely, I accosted one of the two doctors, 'My patient has to be given water from a feeding cup.' He flicked an eye at the distended sac and asked an assistant to bring a cup of water and a spoon. Without taking his eyes off the patient he was examining, the doctor asked me our relationship. I explained. He gave a grunt, presumably of understanding. Some more time elapsed, and the cup and spoon finally arrived, courtesy the second attendant. I remain curious regarding the time of return of the first assistant, assuming he returned at all. I sometimes close my eyes and see him rummaging endlessly through drawer after drawer in search of a feeding cup. Or, may be, he went back to his village and would return after the harvesting season.

The man took a swallow or two again, but this time threw a quick look at me—a fleeting glance with no communication bytes in it, coldly neutral. I knelt down, of course, immediately, to bring our faces on the same level and spoke to him about where he was and why. He stared at the lights in silence. One of the doctors now came to his table and started examining him. After a time he called the other doctor and the two held a consultation. Now, the second doctor placed his stethoscope on the man's chest and listened carefully for a considerable period. He told the first doctor something and went back to the patient he had left. Most of their work seemed to comprise the stitching-up of street wounds. Stone and brick were the chief culprits, but knives were a close second. The patient he went back to had a gash in the abdomen.

The first doctor called me. He was filling up an emergency ticket. Without looking at me, he said, 'The external ugliness is serious but not fatal. The patient seems to be starving for some time and is dying of pulmonary tuberculosis. He must immediately be admitted and treated as an in-patient.'

I was elated, and said, 'Of course'. A tousle headed young face looked at mine for a second. By now I was used to this particular look, a cocktail of contempt, pity and incredulity. I waited patiently for the denouement. It came after he had filled a slip with instructions for taking half a dozen drugs and two tests, one a skiagram of the chest. He wrote on the top of the slip 'malnourished', and, at the bottom, 'Admit as in-patient', inked a rubber stamp on an ink-pad and printed across the ticket: 'Regret No Vacancy' in capitals and 'Please try elsewhere' in small case. Without losing a second, he moved to another table on which a middle-aged man lay with a head wound roughly wrapped in a towel stained red and black.

I was being politely told that in-patient seats were limited and certainly not for vagrants. They were reserved for patients brought by their near and dear ones, who would plead with the doctors and finally use the services of the brokers I had located. I did not know all this at the time, and, had I known of it, would I have engaged a broker to get a vagrant admitted? Who was he to me after all?

The ambulance man took the refusal with equanimity. It was clearly what he had expected. He was expending the day on my education and asked me, 'Now what?'

I looked at the slip of paper in my hand. I understood that this was an official document and permitted me to seek admission for my patient at any public hospital. I could take the slip directly to a doctor in an emergency room without interference from general duty assistants. Even another examination was not required to decide what to do with the patient. My logic leaked like a sieve, but I pulled myself together.

'Let us try another place,' I said.

I really admired our pilot. He made no comment, not even a face. It was pouring again now. With my help he took the stretcher out and skillfully cocooned the man in a sheet of plastic while we transferred the stretcher to its rails on the ambulance. He had fished the plastic out from some corner of the emergency area while I was inside the room wide-eyed with expectancy. The two of us were drenched thoroughly and as the ambulance started and the driver's chamber heated up, vapours rose from our bodies and clothes and misted the windows. The inside of the windscreen had to be wiped clean with a cloth. I was worried about the outside which collected droplets with impunity as the wipers lay impotent at the bottom of the windscreen.

I wondered how he could see the road.

'In rain like this nobody can see. You keep to the middle of the road and put yourself in god's hands. If he is pleased with the world you will see the hulk in front of you in time to dodge it.'

I was not consoled. It was very unlikely that god would be pleased with the world this afternoon.

Once again, the rain stopped as the ambulance reached another public hospital. But, this time the entire area was flooded to my knees, and I floundered alone towards the emergency room, clutching the rejection slip as if it were a passport to tranquility. The driver didn't get down into the murky flood and chewed tobacco pensively, avoiding eye contact with me.

The waters were lazily swirling on the floor of the emergency room and there were two patients to a slab as the people on the ground had to be lifted up when the flood waters came through. An assistant stopped me at the door. I started arguing, waving the slip in my hand. Once again I got the look, the slip was snatched from me, and I was told brusquely to stay outside. For god's sake, was I blind and couldn't I see the situation inside?

In five minutes he returned with another slip and the now familiar ink message. Clutching two slips now, I returned to the ambulance.

The driver spat out the remains of his consoler, gave me a hand up, drove the ambulance to a small eatery on dry land, of the kind made popular by his brethren of the road, and announced, 'I am going for lunch.'

When I didn't stir, he asked, 'What about you?'

'Just some bread, please.' He left while I was still fishing in my pockets for change. He returned in good humour and handed me the bread together with a steaming mug of tea, sweet, strong and almost white with milk. It would barely pass muster as tea, but it seemed just what my insides wanted. I had much trouble in making him accept money, but he gave in finally, and asked me, 'Now what?' I made him repeat what I had surmised—in his experience no hospital admitted dying vagrants.

'But, surely this is not the first time you have been asked to take away a sick vagrant from the road?'

'No, no we are sent for quite frequently, though this is the first time somebody is accompanying such a patient.'

'Well, what do you do?'

'I take him some distance and put him back on the road.' He looked coolly at me after delivering this terrifying statement.

'So, if I just get down and walk away, this is what you will do?'

He shrugged, 'What else can I do?' he said, and, then, 'Wait a minute,' and began to tap his forehead with his forefinger.

He started the engine. 'I have heard of an institution which just might take him in.'

I hadn't realised how hungry and thirsty I was. The tea and bread sent a message of contentment through my body and I must have dropped off for a few minutes. I dreamt I was lying on the pavement on a winter night, shivering and curling myself into a ball in a vain attempt to keep the warmth of my body from draining away into the cold fog outside, orange in the glow of the street-lamps. An ambulance driven by nobody came and stopped by me, and invisible arms lifted me onto a bed in the vessel, on rails. The inside was warmer and I savoured the comfort of the bed till the ghostly ambulance stopped after a few blocks only to bring me out and lay me down lovingly on the roadside. The cold immediately covered me like a blanket, but the sense of being abandoned was itself almost physical, choking my throat with all the sobs I had successfully suppressed since childhood. I tried to plead with whoever was abandoning me but I had no voice and nobody was to be seen. As the ambulance moved off, aghast, I put my hands between my legs to feel for the sac I had half expected to encounter. But there was nothing. Just when the cold was once more piercing my bones the ambulance would reappear and the same play would be enacted again and again till I lost interest in both rescue and abandonment, and no longer felt the cold. At this juncture the big vehicle gave a lurch and, suddenly, I woke with a start and a parched throat. The driver handed me his bottle of water after questioning loudly and thoroughly the legitimacy of the births of all fourteen generations of the driver of a sedan who's dithering on the road had caused the ambulance to lurch.

'By the looks of you I should say you're nursing a fever,' he commented.

Half-clad children were playing merrily on the street and the pavements, crossing our path again and again. The street was a motorist's nightmare, and I had an added worry. Had my philosophical friend once again commended the ambulance and our bodies and souls to his god? I looked furtively at his face, and was reassured. At least his eyes were open. A bolder glance at his hands told me that actually he was steering the vehicle with consummate skill, avoiding lurching youngsters while, all the while, fluently cursing their mothers and grandmothers.

From the main road the street looked like a cul-de-sac. A dirty cat, chased by a pi dog disappeared, however, at the far end, and this told me that the street led to a narrower one. The ambulance stopped. Our destination lay hidden in the narrower street, quite dark in the shade of the buildings on either side. Hovels skirted the buildings, put together with canvas, plastic and hemp. People were gathering fast, materialising as it were from thin air. We dumped our charge on a stretcher and set off, but not before the driver had entrusted the well-being of the ambulance to the leader of the gang of urchins who were the first to surround the vehicle. A shiny coin changed hands, and many words were said, no doubt promises for more—a shrewd sequence of moves because, immediately, the leader turned on his erstwhile followers with an admonition to 'Lay off, or else'.

Through the open doorway could be seen two rows of pallets with an aisle in between. The broad daylight stopped at the entrance and a few kerosene lamps sputtered on the walls, failing signally to dispel the darkness hanging inside the long room like a fog. I entered the infirmary, for so I supposed it to be, and was met by a general lack of curiosity on the part of the occupants of the pallets, emaciated forms mostly, with sunken eyes and jutting cheekbones, the play of shadows giving the illusion of grins and grimaces on skeletal faces. They were dying fast. At the far end a candle burned before a wooden cross.

As my eyes adjusted to the gloom, I made out a desk behind the door. A young woman, dressed in traditional robes, was making entries in what appeared uncannily like a ledger book. She rose courteously on seeing me, and came out into the light to see my patient on his stretcher, shading her eyes with one hand all the while. She bent down and spoke softly to him, but his eyes remained fixed on the heavens. After a time she straightened up and with a sigh motioned us inward, including in her gesture the ambulance man who was chewing on the stalk of a betel-leaf in the shade of the awning of a neighbouring hovel.

I tried giving her the rejection slips, one of which carried the prescription written by the first doctor, but she waved them away and asked us to put him down on any empty pallet. We found an empty place and gently set him down. He stared at the roof.

We walked down to the ambulance and put the stretcher in. The driver winked approval at me and patted my shoulders. Another coin changed hands and he swivelled himself up on his seat and started the engine. The urchins made way, but raised a light cheer of defiance, as a hand came out of the window to wave good luck at me and the ambulance was off, the urchins chasing it out of the neighbourhood, together with the pi dogs that barked their heads off.

Clouds had again gathered in the sky when I entered the room, holding out the slips to the woman at the desk. She asked me to sit down on a stool, and explained to me that they had no provisions for the treatment of the inmates.

'This is a place where their last days can be spent in some dignity and peace.'

She took up a can of water and a small bowl with a long handle. She walked slowly down the aisle giving water to each inmate with much care, wiping off the spilled water with a cloth hanging from her waist. She came to my patient and when water spilled off his pursed lips, sat beside him and tried to make each portion of water very small, until he did take one or two gulps. I walked around with her and when she came back to the desk asked her what I should do with the slips. She told me to fold them down under the pillow in such a way that a part remained exposed.

'Sometimes some agency with provision for treatment visits us and adopts one or two of our inmates.' She was trying to salve my conscience, I thought, so that I would go away and leave them all in peace.

But she would not hold out false hopes. Returning my stare, she told me, 'This happens but rarely.'

'What about food?' I asked.

'Bread and milk,' was the laconic answer.

I rang my friend up on my way back. It was seven in the evening. She was out. What did I expect? Did I think that she would mope all evening because I had stood her up? On Sunday, her set were surely revelling about somewhere, and she had caught up with them.

Next morning, I caught her.

'I am really sorry…'

She interrupted me, 'So, the life and death matter has left you alive. Don't ring me again. If I have something to say I shall contact you.' She cut me off before I could reply.

She generally cut me at college, too. However, she maintained formal and scanty talking terms, limited to preparation for the second part of our degree examinations, though she never came to my house. Unlike what happened in the course of past disagreements, however, I did not hang about in her sight till she deigned to notice me again. This time I went my own way. In fact, I wasn't cut up by her behaviour much, if at all. She sensed this and, quite often, I encountered an appraising stare from her, withdrawn, of course, the moment our eyes met, as if she was perhaps trying to understand my equanimity.

In my heart I found no trace of that infatuation which had almost been an obsession. For a long time I had been at peace only when she was with me. When she was not with me I was forced to wonder where she was and what she was doing. Even otherwise I had been discontented and disturbed by my need for her, which sometimes manifested itself in an intense longing for looking at her eyes. Freedom from her, I had written on a slip, was freedom from want.

The degree examinations came and went. This time we made our separate ways to the examination hall. I returned home, armed with books on Shaw lent to me by the enthusiast in the college. He was writing a book on Shaw's world view, intertwining the themes of Man and Superman *and* Back to Methusela, *and he had asked me to help and collaborate. I had written well at the examinations, I believed, and wanted to pursue postgraduate studies. She also came back and, sometimes, we passed one another on the streets. But she never gave a sign of recognition.*

My results were good, and I was sucked into the fray of admission in the postgraduate course at the university. When I finally emerged bloody and victorious, I started enquiring about her results. She had just scraped through, quite a backslide from her previous results. Even the professors expressed surprise and regret.

She was not to be seen either in the metropolis or the home town. Slowly she faded from the anterior chambers of my conscious mind as other immediate interests took up my mental space. But can we ever be entirely free of those whom we have once loved? A bank of cloud shot across with crimson and orange, a busy crossing, sleepy bylanes, any of these could at an opportune moment bring her back and bitter-sweet memories would flood my mind. Almost a year later, I met my cousin who lived near her father's place during one of my visits home.

'The girl who studied at your college in the metropolis, you remember her?'

'Yes, what about her?'

'O! nothing, she is getting married.'

'An arranged marriage?'

'What else? The groom is very rich, a rice merchant, wholesalers and retail sellers at the local market.'

I wished her well.

I didn't see what more I could do there, and went back to the man. His skin was cold and I opened the neatly folded blanket at the foot of the pallet and arranged it over him. I brought my face close to his and told him that I was leaving and the people here would take care of him. He turned his face and looked into my eyes. The intensity and duration of the stare was unsettling. Suddenly, he began to mutter. I brought an ear close to his mouth. He was saying again and again, 'What place is this? What place is this? What pla…' I was at a loss. How could I say, this is your waiting station for paradise? Then, my eyes fell on the cross. I brought my mouth close to one of his ears, and said slowly in the universal tongue he, too, had used, 'It is God's place'.

He caught my arms with both hands and with one frenzied shove rose to a sitting position on the pallet. He was trembling and I was shaking in his grasp. He continued to bore as it were into my very soul with his eyes, and began to laugh, a mocking, raucous laugh. All eyes were on us. The long room reverberated with the sound of his derisive laughter. Then, the paroxysm passed. He intoned in a slow, tired voice, 'It is of no use.' His body sagged and gently I laid him down on the pallet. His eyes were fixed on the ceiling once again.

The shock drove me along the crowded streets, but I was alone with my thoughts, striding on till I arrived at the river. There was a fine mist on the water through which the giant bridges across the river loomed like ghostly smudges suspended in mid-air. The sun was setting behind clouds in a generally overcast sky.

Next morning I visited the shelter again. The pallet was empty. A different person was at the desk, a young man who could tell me nothing. I wanted to know if the man had died.

'Not necessarily,' said the young man. 'He may have been taken away by some people for treatment.' But the hospital slips were still lying under the pillow.

No, he regretted their inability to keep records or do any paperwork apart from basic accounting. Once we give in to paper, he told me, it will multiply and fill time and space better allotted to men and women. Yes, they had headquarters, but he assured me earnestly, no records from here are sent there. Could I meet the person who was here last evening? Headquarters would know the person but she was a voluntary worker like him and nobody would know when she would come here next, just as he himself didn't know when he would find time again to spend here. No, headquarters would not keep her address, unless she was a regular. Paper, I took the words out of his mouth, multiplies. He nodded, but added darkly that headquarters were talking about keeping files.

I left the anarchist to his fight against paper, and came out of the dark room into the light. Outside, it was quite a sunny morning.

THE HERO

THE MAN'S STORY

I stepped out on the tarmac, a free man. The door behind me clanged shut, muffling the daily sounds of the courtyard I had just left. The road wound on across a lawn within the high outer wall and stopped at a massive iron gate flanked by a guardhouse. A sentry motioned me towards a slatted window in the guardhouse door, where I had to produce my discharge slip. The guard inside had a conversation with the jail gate on an internal telephone, and waved me on. The sentry opened a small door at the bottom of the gate and let me through. I had to double up to pass through the door, and as I straightened I saw the small crowd standing diffidently on the opposite pavement. Behind me rose the fortified eminence of the old prison.

It was a reception committee. My old commissar was there and I was reasonably certain that he had organised the show. There was my wife, looking straight at me, a diminutive woman who knew her own mind. Towering over her stood my son, as unsmiling as his mother. The others were some of our old supporters, mainly from my village. It was almost winter and the autumn harvest was over. As there were no agriculturist landlords or rich farmers to lobby for water to flow down the dry irrigation channels cut by us season after season for subsistence wages doled out as relief, we depended on the god in the sky for water. And as he retired to the warmer underground in winter, our people could not plant any lucrative crops in that season, which explained the turnout the commissar had been able to muster. Had there been work in the fields nobody would have come, I was pretty sure, not even my wife and son. One must first earn one's daily bread.

I attempted a tentative wave of the hand as I stood on the other side of the traffic, waiting for it to ebb. The commissar waved his hand enthusiastically, but the other waves were even more tentative than mine. My wife and son stood impassively. Crossing the road finally, I was caught immediately in an embrace by the commissar. When he released me he was weeping, for the unsung dead, as he explained later in his little address. That one was always sentimental.

Somebody handed a garland to my wife and she came and slipped it around my neck. She had come so close that I could smell her body, a little acridity on a pheromonal background. I noticed that she wouldn't look into my eyes and I read the signs of someone else's presence, but I was prepared for that. No one could be expected to abstain from all real contact with the opposite sex for so long a time. But looking at her, I was overcome by this urge to have her in my arms. I caught her in my arms and kissed her till her body started to respond even though I could feel her attempts at restraint reflecting her ambivalence. She disengaged herself slowly in the middle of a desultory burst of clapping with her heart beating very fast.

The commissar gave a speech, short by his standards. I was a hero of the people, he said. I was the first revolutionary to be raised from the land itself, a person of the people by birth and upbringing, a labourer in the fields of the landlords. I received political training directly from our late, martyred, great leader himself, and organised the people of my community to struggle for their rights. In spite of days of meticulous torture, the State could not make me reveal the real hiding place of the guns kept in my custody as chief of the guerrilla squad operating in our area. Now that I was back I would surely see through the propaganda of various schismatic offshoots from and hostile to the mainstream of the party and work to rebuild the parent organisation to fight against the new landlords. This new breed kept much less land than before but wielded the same power by cornering inputs and markets, and, principally, by managing to have themselves co-opted into the inner sanctums of the hypocritical populist monolith now ruling the country.

Then, I was asked 'to say a few words'. I had much to say, but it would keep. The people of our area, like peasants all over the globe, had arisen before the sky had seen light, and heads had started nodding. My wife stood straight as a tree, as she always did, but her eyes, too, were red and weary from the effort of keeping them open. I declined, claiming an emotional block, and my declaration brought forth the first round of genuine applause.

I touched the commissar's sleeve and made a sign for everybody to rise. He tried to get together a group to raise slogans before dispersal, but we had already started on the long way to the village.

The dirt road was a deeper gash of red in the reddish laterite soil. It was lined by a deep canal, virgin dry. Other such canals could be seen in the far distance. The soil, too, was dry and powdery, and a fine orange smoke hovered above the road. It would have been a Mars-scape had it not been for the fine dark line on the horizon which revealed, as one came nearer, a dark-green forest of trees growing straight up, with brown bark and wide, green leaves, the leaves on the roadward side of the forest covered with the ubiquitous red dust. We skirted the forest to find a stretch of fields sloping gently down to a shallow valley occupied by a dark lake well-known for its clear water and tranquil, mirror-like surface, very definitely an earthscape. A landscape which was entwined with the restless time when, as a growing boy, after back-breaking transfer of rice shoots from nursery to field all day, I would serenade the ebbing colours in the sky with my bamboo flute, so well cut and holed by my half-blind grandfather. He did this without half a glance at his hands, while he recounted tales of the Revolt of the Four Brothers against the colonial power and the landlords and usurers protected by it. He claimed that he was an archer in that unequal fight of bow and arrow against cannon. But we checked and found he had to be more than 110 years old for his story to be true.

Crossing the snug, little valley, we entered a light wood on the other side, capping a little hill. Emerging from the wood, one saw the village laid out on the ground like a picture postcard. As our little party sped down the hill the news spread, and slowly the red path into the village was swamped by the crowds. My commissar was having a field day as he prepared for another meeting.

By the time the talking was done I was thoroughly hungry. Also, though I had had a bath in the morning before leaving the jail, I wanted to immerse myself in water as a sort of ritual cleansing after the years of enforced living in unhygienic and insanitary conditions. Complaints had brought forth what, I suppose, is the standard reply all over the globe, 'You are here for punishment, not to improve your health.' Thankfully, the commissar had overlooked one essential ingredient of village gatherings, namely, sour rice-wine, and the people began to fidget once this was clear to them. So it was that the commissar didn't demur when, instead of making a speech, I announced a date for a subsequent meeting where I would have some important things to say. My wife and son were notably absent.

Having dispatched my ageing leader on his way home, I managed to find some bitter leaf oil in the kitchen and set out for the river on the side of the village away from the wood, wondering whether my wife had kept food for me. On my way I was intercepted by people of my village and other nearby hamlets, and one to one conversations. As we walked they gave me all the information I had missed over the years, commencing even before my incarceration, as a matter of fact, right from the time we went underground. Who died and who were born to whom, who married and who left whom, and why. I had heard of the main facts in prison, but one cannot access the collective understanding with all its overtones, the flesh and blood as it were as opposed to a skeleton, until one has discussed in salacious detail, face to face, the affairs of one's neighbours.

I returned to the aroma of wood smoke, which always evoked in me myriad memories of childhood, my mother boiling rice for all of us, and, once or twice a season, tiny fowl snatched by my father from nearby trees. By the time I reached the wide veranda and washed my feet with the warm water kept for me, the fragrance of cooked rice filled the cottage. My wife came out of the kitchen and set a plateful of steaming rice in front of me on the veranda. A minute later she brought a pot of fowl curry, the bird being a small member of the snipe family. All the time, while I had been thinking that she was with another man, she had been hunting birds in the trees all around with sling shot, weaponry in which she had great facility.

After the meal we sat almost side by side smoking rolled-up green leaves from a plant, akin to tobacco, which every one cultivated for domestic use in our villages. I don't remember when I fell asleep but when I opened my eyes I was lying on the veranda with a blanket around me. There was a high moon in the sky, almost full, and I rose with a conscious effort from a fog of thick layers of sleep to relieve myself in the shadows outside. She was sleeping inside the one room of the cottage, wrapped in moonlight when I lay myself down beside her. She gave a start and awoke to place one hand on my chest. Without thinking, I started to take her in my arms and even though she didn't resist, she disengaged herself promptly, and again placed a hand on my chest. Almost immediately, I drifted into deep sleep.

When I opened my eyes it was still dark, but the birds on the high branches had sensed the coming of light and started a light chatter. I found she had clasped my head to her breast as had been her habit of old. Even my careful movements awakened her and she smiled at me as she almost jumped up. She was always upset if I woke up before her in the morning.

Immediately after ablutions, I changed into tighter and coarser clothing more suitable for working in the field. The moment she saw what I was doing, she came over.

'What do you think you are doing?'

'Going to the labour line.' I had checked yesterday whether the line still stood for hire at the same place as before.

'Do you think I couldn't feed you for a day or two?' A film of tears had formed in her eyes.

'What shall I do the whole day while you are away at work, and so is everybody else?'

'Read those books and journals the commissar brought for you. You were always our window to the world outside.'

'It is too great a burden. You must find somebody younger.'

She sighed and set a pot of stale rice and water, a little salt and a green pepper pod before me.

The others in the labour line were much less comfortable with my presence there than I was myself. Of course, because we are a very polite community nobody said anything directly. But, the jokes I cracked fell flat and the slightly more risky ones didn't raise the expected snigger. Desultory conversation told me that the general view was that a hero, a man the government had thought it worth its money to feed in prison for years, should not stand like meat before the buyer. I, on the other hand, was determined to come out of this false cocoon.

The changes in the social scene were undeniable. As I walked along the high embankment an old man passed me and came back to turn a pair of shrewd, penetrating eyes on my face. With a shock I recognised him—the old landlord who barely escaped with his life in our heyday. We didn't exchange words, and I was surprised to see him proceeding alone without a bevy of attendants and guards. What was even more surprising was that nobody shifted down the side of the narrow embankment to give him right of way. A glow of pride filled my mind. Our people had been defeated. But, nevertheless, we, and, undeniably, the populists, too, working separately and with different aims, had changed the face of rural society.

But, of course, the labour line was still there.

Soon, our populist mini leader was amongst us, picking men for work on his potato fields. Once a labourer like me, he now owned a diesel-powered water pump and had no trouble with winter crops. He also made a tidy sum from hiring out the pump. We had been in the same party when we started, both having been recruited by the old commissar, who had been a schoolmaster at the time. We had since become mortal enemies and people suspected his involvement in my arrest. Always suave, he came forward the moment he noticed me.

'I had heard, old friend, that you had come back. You don't look too bad for an old lag.'

He laughed his booming laugh and slapped my back. Before departing, he came close to me, and, dropping his voice, said, 'If you change your mind about our party, we have endless use for a man of your organising talent.'

I smiled and shook his proffered hand. He had smelt like well-off people do. We here smell of bitter leaf oil all the time.

Time passed. The line thinned slowly. While every buyer had a greeting for me nobody actually considered me for hire.

I could stand it no longer. When a friend, who had come to the jail-gate yesterday, a thrifty farmer, arrived, I shouted out his name.

'Look,' I said, 'I am still stronger than many on the line. The government fed me well, but didn't give me a stash of money to live on for the rest of my life. What is wrong? Do you all want me to die without work?'

There was a silence. Then, at long last, the ice broke. We all dissolved in a paroxysm of laughter. I followed my friend to his field. Now, I owned up to nobody, but prison life had indeed spoilt my body, and I had great trouble lasting the whole day in the fields, and when I returned in the evening my back was numb with pain. I lay prone on the floor, and, my wife, correctly diagnosing the problem, began to massage my back gently, her hands moistened with a little oil, till I fell asleep. It was only a while, before hunger awoke me, but it seemed that I had rested for hours. She fed me steaming rice again, and some sour wine as a soporific. I fell into a dreamless sleep, but not before the thought flitted unbidden through my head. Did she meet him today, and, if so, when and where?

The next evening the pain was less and I could keep my eyes open. My son had sent word that he would be coming with his friends, so I waited on the veranda for them. His wife and little son were the first to appear. My wife and I welcomed our daughter-in-law and grandson in the traditional way and I disbursed the gifts we had kept for the boy. He was a quiet child, brought up traditionally. He knew all the polite responses. But he didn't laugh.

My daughter-in-law was pretty but very quiet, just like her son. I suspected apprehension in the almost furtive glances they threw at my son, and wondered if my son's aloofness and hauteur were responsible for their unusual silence. In fact, the quietness of mother and son made me so uneasy that I was glad when they moved into my wife's orbit.

The men who came with my son described the prevailing political milieu. Our party had broken into fragments, most of which owed their existence to the ego of a person or a small group. Every fragment came to the people it identified to be prospective supporters, and spoke against the other fragments and their leaders. Their political activity was really a search for recruitment alone, their polemics often mere personal attack.

My son's friends were men we hadn't met or won over by propaganda or argument, they were enlisted by the idea made concrete by the movement which swept through their lives. They wanted something great, something to live and, perhaps, die for. A small, inbred group was hardly an improvement on village politicking. They thought the hero would have something momentous to suggest. At the same time, they felt that the hero, being located in their area, would have a suggestion which would as well be of practical use to them.

I told them that I would talk of these matters if they wanted to, after the first meeting where I would place before everybody some things I wanted to say. They were disappointed, but were ready to play along with me. My daughter-in-law served sour wine in cups made of leaves, held together with pieces of dried, hard stalk. I enquired in detail of how land had been passing out from the hands of the old landlords and into the hands of the new elite whose power stemmed from connections with the ruling party and the government, and how production methods had changed over the years I had been away. Hired tractors, power tillers, and oil-driven water pumps had supplanted the bullock and the hand pump, so that, next to land, the availability of cash and credit had become important, a close second in some areas. Apart from all this was the ever-present forest all around, the villages, being, in reality, clearings in the forest, so that the villagers considered the forest and all its produce to be theirs. As the government essentially considered the same to be theirs, to give away as they liked to big business, together with mineral rights, there was scope for severe disagreement and tension. I wanted to know the severity of this conflict.

The commissar had arranged evening meetings in different villages. Not only were the meetings a physical strain on my ageing body which could just about cope with the daily labour, they were a disappointment to the old man, as everywhere I said the same thing—come to the meeting where I will say what I have to say, meanwhile tell me what you think. He was too much of a democrat to tell me what he would like me to say, and thought, I could tell, that I was giving too much importance to this complaint I heard among our supporters everywhere about small group pettiness. In my previous avatar as acolyte, his disapproval, however elliptically expressed, would have stopped me in my tracks. But, I had learnt the hard way that commissars make mistakes which have far-reaching consequences on lives and courses of action. They, too, needed to learn to consider and weigh, without switching on a rejection mode, views perhaps radically different from their own, but emanating from their own people, those whom they commonly classified as followers.

Everywhere I went, my eyes roved, trying to locate the elusive wraith that had in him the spark which had drawn away my wife. I had weighed the possibility of someone in the village, but ruled it as being so improbable that it was impossible. For one, I knew and had refreshed my knowledge of the form of all the starters, and, then, again, nobody in the village, except my son, had shown any signs of keeping something from me.

Considering what I was saying everywhere, it was just a matter of time before other fragments sent feelers. The go-betweens were chiefly inconsequential people. The main competitor of my old commissar's fragment, in our area, was the first to send an important man, a friend from the time we were young blades flaunting our kills from the hunt. An orphan, he had the benefits of a mission school education, and became the youngest commissar in the unified party, one of the few, however, who came from our ranks.

He laughed his disarming laugh as we embraced. I made him sit on the veranda. My wife welcomed him with her graceful signature and gave us sour wine and popped rice. She sat a little distance away from us as he started on his version of the splits in the party and why he, another recruit of my old commissar, had ended up in a different formation. I listened politely, but he was uncomfortable, sensing perhaps my aloofness. The moment he faltered, I said, 'Old friend, I am in no formation. I accompany my old commissar because he likes it and, also, I have to know what has been going on all around while I lay on my prison bunk thinking out and re-thinking what went wrong.'

'O,' he said, and picked up the conclusion, 'You won't join a formation.' In silence he digested this for some time. My wife was staring into the far distance, and I drummed my fingers soundlessly on the floor.

'What are you without a party?' he asked.

'A nonentity, almost as much or as little of the nonentity I would continue to be in a party in which I had no voice.'

'You know this is not the defining characteristic of a party, all parties are not like this. For example, didn't you have a voice in the old party?'

'I had a voice but no one listened to it.'

'This is unfair to the martyred leader. You, of all people, say this? You, to listen to people like you and mainly you in person, he braved a dying condition and white terror and came to the nearby town and spent hours of extreme danger in a workman's flat.'

It was my turn to be silent as disturbing memories churned my mind. I seemed finally to understand a lot of things. My wife was still there, motionless.

'Old friend, yes, I was there and you were there. The leader was brave, if nothing else, and a great visionary with the courage to talk of his dreams and make others dream the same dream. But he listened to me only for confirmation of his vision. So long as this came he was attentive and receptive, smiling the smile we so loved, but his brows knit in the frown, too, we knew so well, when what I was saying went against his vision and his plans. He was on the look-out for echoes, old friend, otherwise why was my criticism deleted from the official account of the day's meeting in the following party letter?'

He was uneasy and excited, 'Don't live in the past, feeding on old grudges.'

'On the contrary, all I am worried about is the future.'

Nothing jelled after this exchange. We fell into casual talk about what old acquaintances were doing, my wife joining in when she knew the people we were talking about. After politely declining an equally polite invitation to a light supper, he rose to go. We shook hands and he walked carefully down the rough pathway out of the cottage. My wife had picked up the lamp and walked before him to set him on the way to the embankment. I remembered he had night sight defect. I sat in the dark staring at the stars as the two figures lighted up by the lamp disappeared around a bend. The crickets kept up a low buzzing. I had understood whom she had been seeing. As is the wont of man I tortured myself picturing them kissing each other hurriedly.

She hummed a tune as she set supper down and called me. It was a tune from our youth and the song was an intensely romantic, a song of love lost and found, which wrung my heart fearfully and I feigned sleep. She sat down beside me and ruffled my hair. The smell of her body unsettled all the queries and speeches I had prepared while she was returning with the lamp. As I turned helplessly to her, she lay down and welcomed me. As I rushed in, she shuddered. My hunger satiated, she caressed my face with her long fingers till I fell into a light sleep. As I woke up, she coaxed me to have supper and wash myself. Waves of sleep swept deliciously across me as I finally curled under the blanket she had laid down. The last thing I remembered thinking was she had co-operated but not responded. I didn't know when she had come in and when she moved out, but I found her singing again in the morning, this time an adaptation in our language of a saucy song of young love from a popular film. The prison had been reverberating with it for the last couple of years and she smiled as I joined her in low volume, providing, though, more of a supporting background to her highs than an accompaniment. Then, to test her, I started a song of a peasant couple who joined the movement, another haunting melody which was popular in our parts. She caught the lows skillfully and without inhibition.

The day finally came. A stage had been set up with bamboo and jute sacking, and the electrician was busy fixing the wiring for lights, microphone and loudspeaker. A few chairs had been placed before the dais, the rest were dotted about the huge open-air natural auditorium. Children played musical chairs in high glee. As the sun set and the lights came on, people started to gather. The old commissar materialised with a band who sang people's songs, and started the meeting. It was planned that after a few songs he would speak and finally I would take over. I had tried to protest feebly on two counts. First, I had told everybody that I would speak. While this did not preclude anyone else from speaking, the idea certainly had been to present me alone. Secondly, the old commissar, however widely acceptable, was the member and, in fact, high priest of a particular formation, and leaders of other formations might want to speak in rebuttal. My protests were not very strident because, after all, they were paying for the show. The old commissar said it was quite natural that in this area, the two of us would speak, and it was unlikely that other leaders would come. He proved right on both counts. Even the friend who had been the youngest commissar was absent.

The old commissar spoke briefly, cleverly interweaving the separation of his fragment from the old party with, what were to him, the highlights of my life and ended with an exposition of my heroism in the face of torture.

The field was packed when he called me to speak. There was applause especially from the younger sets. I thanked the old commissar for his kind words. I referred to the group meetings I attended after my release and the prevailing dislike of the small group mentality which had severely curtailed our strength to intervene in important matters. I spoke of the current situation in which all political parties were duping the people, and some actively oppressing them. I asked them what was necessary to be done at such a juncture, and said that actually this was the question I had to face at all meetings. Now, people wanted an answer from me because they considered me to be a hero. But, there were no heroes in reality, except that people made them so. People must forget about heroes and think for themselves. 'Take my own case', I said. 'I had become a hero because of a misunderstanding. I tried hard to withstand police torture and put up with it for two days, but I broke on the third day. My mind was not in my control and I heard my mouth telling them where and with whom the guns were hidden.'

There was a sound as if dammed waters were rising and swirling. I continued, 'The police beat that person mercilessly till he took them to the hiding place.' Shouting had started, especially at places with a concentration of people supporting other fragments. I had to shout practically at the top of my voice, 'But the hiding place was empty. No one knows what happened, and now the custodian is also dead.'

I was speaking almost to myself now, there was such a roar and a rush to the dais. I had deprived the people of a hero, and they were baying for my blood. I was saying, 'Everybody including the police were convinced that I had misled them, and torture continued till I was half dead and they gave it up as a mystery…' when somebody yanked out the microphone.

As people were standing up I didn't see the counter-movement. A band of young men, with my son among them, had slowly but firmly proceeded to the dais and now formed a protective cordon around me, as I climbed down, with a hand each on an axe pushed into his waist. I didn't know how long they would have been able to stem the violent tide, but they kept their heads. From the beginning of the melee, two of them, one a woman, tried hard to put the lights out, and finally succeeded. In the dark, the woman ran to me and dragged me away from the dais. It was my wife. I was too dazed to find a safe way out, but she tied a cloth around my head in such a way as to obscure a part of my face and led me through gaps between the cottages till we reached my son's house. Having pushed me up into the loft there and locked me in, she returned to our house. Milling crowds reached my house, soon, as I concluded from the noise proceeding from that direction. My son's cottage was deserted. I understood that he had, in advance, shifted his wife and son away somewhere, perhaps to his in-laws' place in a closeby hamlet. The way his little band had intervened in the melee also showed signs of advance planning, and there, sitting in the loft in pitch darkness behind a door, locked by my wife from the outside, to lend credence to the deserted look, I thought about the identity of the person who could have anticipated trouble at my meeting and laid down these contingent plans. The only possibility was the old commissar.

The ruckus was continuing near my house and I feared for her safety and blamed myself for listening to her. I kept my eyes peeled in that direction to catch the first reddish-yellow glow if they torched the roof. I had half made up my mind to climb down and present myself before their anger, when the shouting slowly subsided. I fell into an uneasy sleep, broken continually by the mosquitoes. I dreamt I was crouching in one corner of my prison cell. A man had escaped and the 'mad bell' had been set ringing. This was a signal to the warders to beat up the inmates at will as no accounts were drawn of such incidents if they occurred within the 'mad bell' time. Warders settled individual accounts and I was waiting for the chief warder, the kingpin of all jail rackets and connoisseur of boys in the Imports Room which housed newcomers for a night. He was a bully and because I had stood up to his bluster, time and again, he had me marked. I saw the door of the cell darken as his bulk filled it. The heavy baton was raised, poised above my head. As it started to come down I awoke with a start. She hadn't yet come and I had this nagging thought that perhaps the cessation of noise had meant that they had satisfied themselves by doing her grievous harm, striking at me by proxy.

She came back as I was preparing to come down and led me to our house. We were challenged once. She whispered to me that village sentiment had rallied around and sentries had been put out.

She seemed to be in good spirits and was humming a song of harvest time, a joyous folk tune demanding dancing along. She put out her hands and there on the darkened veranda at midnight we danced, two shadows gyrating around each other in a tightening spiral. When we met she was urgent in her movements and this time there was no holding back.

Next morning, this spirit deserted me as the happenings swirled round and round in my mind. I sprawled against the mud wall of the hut and gazed over the land into the far distance. My wife gave one look and left me alone.

Soon, the old commissar arrived and my wife gave us some wet rice. He had come, he said, to accompany me to the labour line, 'in case'. But the people I met were civil. Some averted eyes but quite a few responded to my nods. The commissar himself was exuberant. Drinking sour wine before we started from my house, he laughed his rare, big laugh, which was almost a roar. 'Well, well, well. So you are a hero after all, with all the patent characteristics of the species, including courage foolhardy to the point of inviting death. Why didn't you give me an inkling beforehand of what you were up to? Didn't you expect the mood to swing towards lynching?' I admitted that I expected a hearing of my case in full. But I was taken aback. The contingent planning was not of his doing.

When he took his leave, he was thoughtful. 'I want to hear your views on the small group syndrome we are suffering from and how to establish a real dialogue between the party and the people, what is that catch phrase you have coined about leadership?'

'The party will lead the people and the people will lead the party.'

'Hmm', he smiled, 'you mix a foggy cocktail of the accursed mysteriousness of your community with the exasperating ellipticity of German dialectics.' He departed, muttering that we would yet walk the roads together. I doubted it, for, as I gazed over the meadows to the shimmering blue of the distant mountain, I realised the toll these last few days had taken of me, especially the run-up to the meeting and its outcome, so sadly miscalculated by me, and a pall seemed to settle on my thoughts.

I was happy, though, for my old mentor. My brush with death at the hands of my compatriots had brought home to the old man my deadly seriousness and he had started rethinking his own position.

The real surprise came in the evening when the full band of my son's friends turned up to continue their sessions with me. We spoke for three hours before she served supper and for two hours afterwards. They were hungry to share my experiences and my conclusions, but they took nothing for granted without discussion and debate. Right at the end they said they wanted me as a teacher. I understood what they wanted was a leader, but 'leader' was a bad word just now. I shut my eyes and thought it through. I was tired and this push was all I was capable of. The old commissar would hammer them into a cutting edge. The rest was up to them.

I opened my eyes and nodded. That is how we say 'No'. Perhaps, they saw the tiredness in my eyes, for they didn't insist.

With my wife, I tried to talk of my friend, the youngest commissar and whether they had any relationship. She put one finger on my lips, and that remained another unanswered question.

THE WOMAN'S STORY

I saw him sketch an incomplete wave of the hand across the traffic and my heart went out to him, as always, in a sweep of protectiveness. He was diffident, uncertain of his welcome, as he looked into my eyes. I don't know what he saw there but he kissed me, an act in public which was quite uncharacteristic of him and our community. But, if he wanted to imprint his presence on my consciousness, he succeeded. My body was intensely aware of him and I was limp when he released me.

I could feel he understood my trouble and his maturity surprised me. He desisted from taking me at night, but, then, he was also tired and sleepy. Waves of affection overwhelmed me as I looked at his sleeping face, and cradling his head in my breast, I went off to a much deeper sleep than I had been enjoying these years. I must have slept for long as he was already awake when I opened my eyes. I felt ashamed but simply smiled at him before getting up.

He insisted on going off to find work, and, though I wanted him to rest and find his moorings, I had always loved this old independence of his. The movement was in ebb, the party had splintered, the people still angry but only passively so. Everybody wanted to hear his opinion on the lessons to be learnt and what had to be done now. I sensed a great reluctance on his part to act the hero, and when he started to put off discussion till he had his say in public, I started to sense what was eating away at his heart. Even as I admired him, a great fear filled my soul.

I was still a girl when I first became conscious of this man, this boy growing into a man would be a better description, for his dreams were boyish, untouched by the cold hands of calloused experience. His grandfather talked incessantly of the days when all the land and what was above it and underneath were ours, and how the landlord cum moneylender swallowed all of it except the forests which were leased in by the timber and leaf merchants, and, the minerals clawed out by the mine owners, and how our people rose against them and the colonial power at the call of the Four Brothers.

He worked on his father's small plot of land, growing vegetables which his parents and younger brothers sold at different weekly markets. At the hint of the first light, you would see him on the outskirts of the village, assiduously practising his archery. He was one of the best hunters among the younger set. The hunting festival always saw him return from the mountain with an overflowing hunting bag. My brother was a fan of his and a sort of side-kick, and from him I would hear of his exploits. Once, he faced a wild boar, one of the most determined and ferocious fighters of the wilderness when cornered, whom he pinned down for almost an hour till others arrived. Come evening he would wander about the hills and valleys playing the flute. He improvised his own music which ran the full gamut from slow melancholy to sprightly marches, depending on his mood.

He was the dream boy of all the girls of the village. I was haunted by his music which I seemed to hear wherever I went, and his first touch during a collective dance in the harvest festival thrilled me inside out. At the end of the ritual I circled the fire in the middle of the dancing ground in a slow rhythm at first and, then, going faster and faster as the percussionists caught my wildness, until other maidens, who had joined in, stepped out, exhausted and outclassed. He joined me finally and the two of us executed a convoluted series of steps to an ovation which shared our excitement and joy. We became inseparable, walking across the fields hand in hand, his voice intoning like a spell the substance of his wandering dreams, a march of the people to reclaim their land. One of his favourite places was a wide ledge on the slopes of the hill rolling down to the valley of the lake.

The idyll ended when his father died and the landlord sent his bodyguards to occupy their land, on account of debt purportedly incurred by his father, though on his death-bed the old man had categorically told him that he owed nothing to anybody. He resisted the guards till all of us arrived and crowded around them. They, then, brought out automatic pistols and withdrew. At night a large armed police party came and arrested him, dragging him over the stubble in the fields and the broken paving stones of the pathway to the main road, where stood their black van. An armed detail was left at the plot. Of course, they retired at night to the landlord's house and accompanied the landlord back to the plot in the morning. He ordered his men immediately to till the plot for illegal poppy cultivation. He started working for wages on other people's land when he returned from custody, and, did two things which I understood he had thought out to the full during his days of enforced idleness in jail. With his first week's wages in hand he asked me whether I would marry him. For answer, I kissed him full on the lips. He, then, approached my parents, who were less than overjoyed, having seen his status change in a month from landholder to wage-labourer. But, knowing me, they created no trouble.

Second, he sought out the old commissar and in six months the two of them patched together a labour union. The landlord tried to kill both of them, and he was mentally and by temperament unsuited for a life of evasion by careful planning, and would have fallen, had it not been for the wily old commissar who gave him strict rules to live by. The landlord sent men to burn our house at night but we were already keeping sentries. The arsonists were caught and the younger men doused them down with the paraffin they themselves had brought. He arrived just in time to prevent the final setting of a lighted match to their shaking bodies. The police came to their rescue and the officer said he had orders to arrest him and others for attempted murder. We understood that he was hesitating because we were armed with picks and axes and quite plainly determined to resist arrest. Finally, the secretary of the labour union, an older man, told the officer to tell his superiors that any use of force would lead to a strike. A lot of two-way talk over the wireless phone resulted in a decision not to arrest anybody, but a police camp was set up in the landlord's house.

Over the next few years, I had grown up into a woman but his mind remained that of a boy, filled with misty yearnings, and without clear ideas about how they could be fulfilled in the real world. He would often rush into projects without thinking them through and did not have an objective assessment of his own capabilities, propensities, and limitations.

In this way was he drawn into the movement for an autonomous province for our community. With his friends, he brought a whiff of fresh air into the musty corridors of intrigue and horse-trading which characterised the caucuses of this movement. Our house became a bee-hive of activity with people having dinner without prior intimation, staying the night, leaving in the middle of the night. Meetings were commonplace, some all-night affairs. Quite a few of his leaders were well-off people of ill repute. I didn't like their ambiguous speeches and shifty eyes. One or two tried baby-talk with my son, who was going to a proper school, and intensely disliked their patronising sibilations. But, at the time, my husband couldn't see through their false exteriors.

He became an instant celebrity when he stood for election to a parliament seat as a candidate on the plank of a separate province, and won.

Within a month he was back from the capital city with a thundery countenance, refusing all callers.

At night, he told me, clutching my body like a drowning man, 'This party which made me a candidate is selling our votes to the ruling party at the rate of a hundred thousand per vote against the motion of no-confidence brought by the opposition.' I couldn't help bursting into laughter at his lost air.

'How much were you supposed to keep?'

'Twenty per cent.'

'O that is why you are dejected. How much would have satisfied you?' I couldn't help teasing him.

He understood, and started laughing. Slowly the tenseness left his soul. Thankfully, no party could form a stable government and fresh polls were ordered. This time the national parties sent feelers. But he wouldn't rise to the bait again.

Meanwhile, an armed movement, mainly of the peasants, had started, challenging the political power of the landlords and big businessmen, and the old commissar roped in all his recruits on the side of the peasants. My husband joined the movement, as did a childhood friend of his, an orphan, who had been taken away by the padre to a residential school run by the mission, and had now returned. Brave and enterprising, the two of them soon shot into prominence, my husband as the leader of an armed squad and his friend as a political interpreter of the communications of the central leaders to the peasants.

While my husband was busy leading his squad, the government sent an army of occupation. Our house was one of the first to be visited. The officer barked an order and two soldiers came forward,

'Where is he?' he asked. I said, shielding the small, trembling body of my son with my own, 'I don't know'. The officer gave a nod and a soldier struck me on my protruding belly. An intense, searing pain tore my insides. I sat down. The last thing I remembered was the feel of little arms around my neck. When I came to, I saw the elderly women of the village all around me. My head was in the lap of my mother and I was wet all through and barely covered with a sheet of cloth.

'You have had a miscarriage,' my mother whispered. 'You have been cleaned and washed. If you can get up, I can dry you up and you can wear something proper'. My son slowly came and stood before me. I held out my arms and he came into them. He has never since laughed, at least I have never heard him. I had not been singled out specially. All through our area our men and women were tortured and raped, more for punishment than for extracting information.

We had no option but to fight, and, fighting, we learnt to laugh again and enjoy each day as a precious gift which might not be repeated. I left our house with the boy, and, indeed, our village, because the army sent search parties often. Once I narrowly escaped rape by running into the forest, where the miscreants didn't dare enter. I went to the village that my mother belonged to, and started living with my brother who was a bachelor and spent most of his time down in the lowlands, where wage labour on the fertile, well-irrigated land, yielding three crops a year, was available all the time. My husband occasionally visited me at night and I found him disturbed and much in need of succour. He was missing his flute, he was missing me, and he was missing the boy. The big child in him was intoxicated by the role of the champion of the people, but narrowness of the warrior's life in the underground was testing the limits of his mental strength.

Sometimes he came with his mission school friend. I liked this man with laughter wrinkles around his eyes, who seemed unscathed by the life of the professional revolutionary, but was uneasy at his frank admiration, especially when he arrived alone, which happened frequently, this being his native village. But he was decorous, visiting me only by day when he came alone. I was relieved when my brother returned to join the movement. The police were not aware of him and the party kept it that way, so that he could be given special, secret tasks. I kept house for him and he lived the life of an ordinary labourer. The villagers, of course, knew everything, but it was a working people's village and every one supported what had now become a revolt.

The squad led by my husband targeted the landlord of our old village. His house servant had brought the news that he would be skirting this village while returning from the market town. Of course, there was a police camp in his house and he always took four armed guards when he travelled. The pathway was close to the forest at one point and this was where the guards would be wary. So, the squad would wait a little beyond this point where a bend would keep them out of the view of the advancing party. The path went over a culvert at this point and the ruins of a brick kiln would offer ample cover. I was given a special task. I was to work on the fields on one side of the pathway, with a cloth around my hair to obscure my face, which was not unknown to the landlord. When the landlord's party approached the bend I was to stand up with my back to the pathway.

Everything was set. The landlord's party walked briskly past what they considered to be the danger point and relaxed when nothing happened. Just before the bend, the guards stopped to light cigarettes offered to them by the landlord. The men of the squad were invisible behind bushes, inside the culvert and within the ruins of the brick kiln. I stood up. I was quite far off, but in the still air the ribald remarks of the guards wafted on to me. Then, suddenly, there were shouts. I lay down flat within the crops, with only a peep way for my eyes. The men, faces rendered unrecognisable by streaks of black paint, jumped on the guards with axes. The rifles of the guards were useless in such close combat. They didn't carry side-arms and had not fitted bayonets to the guns. The encounter was over in five minutes. The men walked away with the guns. Nobody stirred on the pathway, and I walked through the fields back to the village. The village knew nothing. I waited till the first news arrived. Four people had died and one was in hospital in a critical state. The police were arriving in force at the spot and would start pouring into the villages any moment. The men and boys, including my brother, left the village and as I had foreseen he pressed on me to leave. On close scrutiny some spy would recognise me. I left with the boy. Later, I learnt it was the landlord who survived.

The armed forces razed to the ground all the huts of the working people in our native village and arrested everyone they found, old men and women, children, women heavy with child. A huge contingent raided villages in a wide arc around this point, raping women and beating up children. Some members of the squad were caught in the dragnet. My husband and his friend were sent outside the arc to develop newer areas. My brother returned home, sick with a mortal illness. An uneasy calm set in, and my son started going to school again, though, time and again, there were long stretches of enforced holiday. I was now the breadwinner.

A rustle in the night awakened me. He was standing in the shadows just beyond the fencing around the house. I ran into his arms and we made love furiously. There was a hopelessness about his haste, as if the world was ending tonight. After awakening my brother I went inside the hut and stayed with the boy behind locked doors, as he had asked me to do. After half an hour, my brother knocked on the door. He was covered in sweat. I looked all around as I dried his fevered body and brought dry clothes for him to put on. There was no one to be seen. My brother fell asleep almost immediately.

I came down to the courtyard and inspected it thoroughly. I found what I had feared I would find, and sat on the veranda thinking about my husband fondly, the big, brave child. He had sought to enter the world he dreamed of and I feared that he found it was an adult's world, and was not prepared for meeting the demands it made on him. I knew what would finally happen, and what I did was to compensate for this beforehand.

Soon afterwards he, and then his friend, were arrested. We sent his mother to the police lock-up, and she brought back the news that they were both being tortured mercilessly. I left the house with the boy, for my brother was in no condition to travel. I ruffled his hair and he looked at me with swimming eyes. Both of us knew we wouldn't meet again. Within a day or two armed forces came and dug up the entire courtyard, and when they found nothing, they took out their ire on my poor brother, who died within a month.

The movement ebbed away. The landlord of our native village recovered and sent out news that his fields were untilled and he wanted labour to return. He guaranteed there would be no police action, and he was ready to give each prodigal a small house-building loan. I came back with my son who had suddenly started growing into a little giant and both of us started daily labour.

Years passed. My husband had become a hero in the collective mind and was lodged in a high security prison, too far for us to visit regularly. In fact, I went there only once, when the news came that he was very ill. Both of us were greatly affected, and he told me not to come again as police spies were watching me intently.

My son married early, and I was already a grandmother when prisoner release started in ones and twos. His friend sought me out after his release and started visiting me frequently. I found him more mature than my husband, humorous, illusion less and practical. I enjoyed his company and, why should I deny it, I had been starved of male admiration for too long a time. We became lovers but were very discreet. I didn't want any unpleasant news to disturb my husband in prison. My son understood what was happening, and didn't approve of it, not because of any sense of loyalty to his father, whom he had forgotten as an individual, but first, because, he was intensely possessive about me, leaving pointedly if his father touched me in his presence, and, second, for some reason, he had never liked this friend of ours. However, in our community, privacy is respected, and he quietly set up a separate household without acrimony.

When my husband returned, I discovered to my consternation that the chemistry between us was returning with every passing day. Then, his friend came to see him. They had a debate so intense that I think they forgot my silent presence. I found that my husband had thought out our mistakes and rejected the politics of splits while his friend was caged in today's lore. As the argument proceeded I began to understand certain facets of the latter's character better. What I had admired as a lack of illusions I suddenly saw was a lack of commitment and his practicality another name for a lack of principles. My husband had matured while retaining his vision of empowerment of the people. And the more I realised the terrible sincerity driving him, the more I understood his peril. By the time the argument ended my infatuation with his friend was over. Deliberately, I accompanied the departing visitor to the main pathway with a light. He turned to me the moment we were out of sight of the cottage, and couldn't believe the liaison was over. I was shocked to find that he was quite agreeable to carry on the affair garnished with the usual sordid subterfuges. As a result I was perhaps harsher in my dismissal of him than he deserved and he never spoke to me again.

But he was out of my mind the moment I turned around. I had much to do. That night my husband took me but I was so consumed with fear for him that I was not fully with him. The moment he fell asleep, I ran to my son. His disapproval of my conduct had made him adopt a certain laconic impassivity with me, and, also, he had never been close to his father. I saw him looking mockingly at the older man more than once, after his release, and I didn't find it easy to seek his help. But there was no one else I could turn to.

I entered the courtyard and crept to the outside wall of their room and whispered his name sharply while scratching the wall, an old signal between us in the dangerous days. Just recalling those days sent a pang through my heart. After sometime he looked out from the window, through which I saw framed, behind his head, the frightened faces of his wife and son. I made a reassuring gesture to them and beckoned out my son. He was not overjoyed to see me, but I saw concern in his eyes as I explained to him what I thought his father was about to do.

Everybody knows what happened after his momentous speech and how we saved him. I took him through gaps between cottages and backyard jungles to our son's house, and locked him up. While hastening to our house I heard a roar coming closer and closer. I had to reach the house before this flood, or the plot would be discovered, and I ran faster and faster till my chest seemed to be caught in a vice-like grip and the pain made me bite my lips till the blood came.

As I fell on the veranda, panting, my prone figure would seem to be weeping in great gusts.

'Stop the playacting and tell us where he is,' went a harsh voice on and on, till I jumped up in rage. 'I don't know and wouldn't tell you if I knew.'

'Why, you heard what he said.'

'Yes. Now, look at yourselves. Since the white terror began, have none of you committed even one act for which you are secretly remorseful?'

A great silence fell on the gathering.

'The difference is that you keep it snugly hidden and he has torn his heart out and shown you the lacerations in it.'

'Why did he have to make a fool of us who believed in him? He need not have talked about what he did in public. The difference is that he is a flasher and we are not.' Others tried to shut the speaker up. I held up a hand. When he had finished, I resumed, 'You left him no choice—you made a hero out of him, a construct of your mind, and ballooned him into the sky. He had to tell everyone the truth so that he could free himself of your absurd need for a hero and come down to the earth. And because he has pricked dead this balloon of a hero you built, you are angry with him. It is yourself you should be angry with, each of you.'

Burdened with their own secrets, they all turned back slowly, some alone and others in groups. Some who knew us of old came and muttered words of some sort of an apology before they left. When they were all gone my son came and sat with me till the excitement slowly drained out of my system and walked with me to his house. We were just in time. The man was so worried about me, he had climbed down from the loft and was making ready to break out of the locked cottage. My son had disappeared, and, hand in hand, we returned to our old house.

The next evening my son came with his friends to offer him the palm. I was on tenterhooks. The man had forgotten he was a bird of the sky. Making music and singing made him happiest. He was too romantic to be a good revolutionary, and too democratic to be a leader. He couldn't even foresee what effect his speech would have on the multitude. And constant dealing with such things so foreign to his nature had already bred tiredness in his soul.

But, he turned down their offer, and looked intently at the relief easily visible on my face, as if to ask, 'Are you satisfied, then?' Well, I was.

THE SON'S STORY

My friends didn't understand why I showed no special enthusiasm on learning of his impending release. I knew he was no hero, although this was not what I held against him. It required an unearthly soul to cope with the ingenuity of small people bent on using the weapon of pain to bring down a human being to a state of zero dignity. To last this out would require the resources of a much bigger person, a saint and not a mere hero, and certainly not someone posing as one. What took away my respect for the man was his hypocrisy, the fact that he permitted people to think of him as a hero. He always had a little of the humbug in him, even in his fighting days, and I never could understand what my mother saw in him.

As I waited in front of the jail gate I was disturbed to find that my reason was not softened with the slightest touch of filial feeling, and I wondered why. Was it some shortcoming in my affect or the shuffling of all priorities in the mind by the times we lived in? So, when he waited helplessly for the traffic to dry up, with half a wave of one hand accentuating his uncertainty about the degree of his welcome, I was relieved to find a certain compassion welling out from compartments of my mind so long concealed even from myself. Jail had taken away quite a few teeth and much of the bush of hair, I remembered, sitting on his head, and deep lines of suffering and concentration had been etched into his face. Why, he is almost an old man, I thought and, contrary to my apprehensions, without much of a fancy for the exchange of meaningless speeches. Instead, he kissed my mother, and quite hard, too, something not really done in our community in public. I understood immediately that he was making a statement to my mother, and, for the first time, a grudging admiration for him flitted through my mind, although, as always, I resented the air of proprietorship with which he touched her. He won light applause from our little crowd, too, mainly I suspect for not starting a speech. He started for his village, even as the old commissar was trying to organise some slogan shouting.

My friends insisted on meeting him, in spite of my disparagement of their plan. They had this idea that he must have summed up his experiences during his long stay in prison and might have something significant to say on the current situation. As I couldn't divulge the real reasons for my reservation, I was forced to let them accompany me on my formal visit home to introduce my wife and son to him.

He surprised me. He was only interested in listening to us, a new experience with a so-called leader, and politely avoided airing any opinions. On being pressed, he named a date when he would say something publicly, and if we wished to discuss things with him after hearing what he had to say he would meet us again. He was hungry for information about the changes, social and political that had been occurring over all these years and asked many questions.

He caused another ripple of astonishment when he started work as a daily labourer. There was a feeling that it was not proper for a hero to sell his body, but the younger people were glad that he was back to his moorings. Somehow, they felt more secure with such a man.

All in all, he seemed eminently unsuited to the role of hero, and I carried back with me the new feeling that he, too, was ill at ease with this mantle and his public meeting was concerned with laying it down. I was pleased with him on the whole, especially and paradoxically because he had started to woo my mother again. She needed to be extricated from an unfortunate intimacy with another former leader, a friend of both of them. This individual was a self-seeker, a seeker after power, loyal only to himself, with, however, an exterior presence and conduct carefully cultivated to impress people. I thought less of my mother for joining a line of women who had failed to see through him.

The day of his meeting drew near. It would be a crowded occurrence. The reluctant hero was taken by the old commissar from village to village. Everywhere he announced the date of the meeting, and made it clear that only after this would he be in a position to discuss the problems and tasks of the day. Expectations rose and political rivals of the old commissar also sharpened their knives. There would be questions, if not heckling.

One night, there was a light scratching sound from the wall near our bed and someone whispered my name. My son was the first to hear it, and he awakened me silently. As I sat up, I recognised the signal. It was my mother. My wife was awake by this time, and was thoroughly frightened, as was the boy. After reassuring them, I came out to meet my mother. She said, 'Your father is going to face death tomorrow. He will tell the people he divulged the hiding place, and they will kill him.' I was not surprised. We made our plans. While accompanying her back to their house, I asked her, 'Did he tell you his plans?'

'No. But I am certain this is what he will do.'

I sighed. Looking at her full in the face, I asked her, 'Have you rid yourself of the other?' She gave me a reproachful glance, which meant, 'Yes, but mind your own business.'

I waited to see her go on her way, but she turned back and slowly approached me. I put out my arms and she settled in them.

'You knew, didn't you?' she asked me.

It was my turn to answer with a glance. She stood up, still waiting, and I added, 'The door had a crack and, putting my eyes to it, I saw you dig the heavy, plastic package out and remove it from the courtyard. After a long time, you returned and filled up the trench and swept the fill till it was plane.'

Her voice broke, as she said, 'If a man doesn't know what he can do and what he cannot, his friends must help him.'

'Where did you bury them?' I had to know.

'I will tell you when you need them.' She had composed herself after the moment of weakness.

What happened at his meeting is now part of our folklore. After everything was quiet, my mother took me to let him out from my house where she had locked him in after the meeting. I suddenly had an attack of shyness and withdrew into the shadows. As I watched them walk away, hand in hand, I discovered that my animosity towards him was shrinking.

Early next morning my band of young men gathered at my house. They wanted to talk or, rather, listen to him that very evening. We offered him the leadership and he didn't accept it. My disappointment was tempered with certain gladness. My mother, no doubt, wanted him to refuse.

As I left him after the session, an impulse made me ask him, 'Have you anything to say to me?'

He looked into the far distance for a long time, as was his wont. Then, he turned to me with a smile and said, 'Talk to your son.'

Slowly, I shook my head in that gesture which meant 'Yes' while the guns rested comfortably in oil, somewhere, waiting for me quizzically.

MUSIC AND SENESCENCE

From his diary

Usually I had little difficulty walking on flat land. The pain caught up with my knees on the staircase. Going up was more strenuous because of my narrowing arteries, but coming down was the riskier enterprise because my knees sometimes tried to give up the burden of keeping me upright as bone squeezed past bone in the drying joints.

The moment I left my bed, as the first rays of light came in, to let my legs bear my weight was a bad one. As I stood on the floor and straightened my back, a sharp pain shot through the knees, and, as I now knew, I had to press down on the bed to prevent buckling at one knee or the other. Then came the worst part of the day. I had this habit of squatting on my feet while washing myself, and the knees felt as if they would burst out of my legs. When I stood up again I rested a while, savouring the delicious sense of the absence of pain.

I would not have accepted the contention that the absence of a sensation was a sensation unless I had experienced it myself. My attention has of late, started wandering in unfettered pleasure during the precious moments while the relief lasts, and the idle thought crossed my mind, that, quite possibly, what was being declared to be an absence of sensation was actually coloured by a flood of neurotransmitter rewards at appropriate neural junctions.

My friend the surgeon had suggested well planned exercises, one particular sequence to be repeated 300 times a day, and dubious drugs somewhere between magical medication and food supplements, and told me that what I actually needed was knee replacement. I refused surgery because what I dreaded above all was a failed operation and a grounded existence in which I would be dependent on others for arranging disposal of the waste from my body and cleaning my orifices, day after day. No one can keep on loving a leaking bag of offal. This I had seen at close quarters.

My uncle had suffered a cerebral stroke and consequent motor loss in all four limbs. At first my aunt and cousins vied with one another in serving the invalid. After a month the married cousins proposed the employment of professional care-givers with equal cost-sharing all round. After two months this proposal was accepted. Only my aunt could not be spared, because my uncle refused to let paid nurses, male or female, clean his private parts. The enforced invalidity was a great burden on his mind which slowly disintegrated under the strain, and his decision not to let thorough cleaning proceed unless it was carried out by his wife was considered at the time to be the demand of a sick mind, though to me now, as it had seemed to me then, the demand was sane and rational. That it might have been too much for the care givers from the family itself was another matter.

My aunt, however, never pleaded any excuse and considered her chores to be the atonement for unknown crimes and criminal thoughts.

Whenever I returned to the city I helped her out, silently witnessing the decline of civilised discourse in the household. After a year, my uncle was noticeably worse. He needed help even to sit up. His mind retained only a tenuous hold on certain aspects of reality. Incontinence had set in and he needed a urine bag and diapers. Fitting them on was a daunting task. He strained to move his limbs, his face growing red and the great blood vessels throbbing at his temples, and he screamed in frustration, tears collecting on his face in pools before running down his neck to wet the bed clothes.

My aunt loudly complained about her fate, and cursed her long-dead father who had mercilessly pulverised her first love to marry her off to his chosen groom, now this living corpse. Then, she took to slipping off every other afternoon and my curiosity was aroused. One afternoon when a cousin's wife could be requested to sit in the invalid's room, I followed my aunt out of the house. To my surprise, she walked briskly to the main traffic junction nearby and turned into a jeweller's shop specialising in precious and semi-precious stones. I followed her in only to lose her. There was nobody inside the tiny, dark shop except a middle-aged salesman who stared at me, eyes widening and fingers readying over the red emergency button which rang a bell inside the nearest police station.

'Where did the woman go?'

The salesman pointed to a door with a nameplate, which I had missed in the gloom. On the wall beneath the nameplate was a poster. 'SEE THE WORLD, SEE THE LIFE', it shrieked in bold lettering.

She confessed, when we came out of the musty smell pervading the shop, that because she, an addict of romantic films, could no longer be spared even an hour for herself, she had to discover this video parlour selling very tame blue film shows, fifteen minutes ago. I had noticed from some time back that she was wearing on her fingers a conglomeration of rings featuring semi-precious stones, but had failed even to imagine their potency as camouflage.

'Are you staying another three days?', she asked timidly when she found that I wasn't shocked, but, rather, behaved as if watching fifteen minutes of blue film show every other day was an unremarkably

pedestrian activity. It transpired that a sequel was due on the third day, but it would take half an hour.

I filled in for her.

With time, she slowly became quiet and tears streamed down her face whenever she looked at her husband. She no longer screamed. Instead, she regularly cooked his favourite dishes and fed him with her own hands. Quite often, she fasted from daybreak to sundown, and, during the visit of the physiotherapist, shut herself up in the small room which housed the sacred images she worshipped. But, uncharted territories in her mind having bobbed up before my eyes, I wondered very much what prayers she offered to her deities.

One afternoon, after another six months or so, I was sitting outside my uncle's room reading a daily newspaper. My aunt came out of the room and stood silently at a window overlooking the busy road outside. After some time she turned. Her eyes were wet, and she started sobbing in great, silent gusts which racked her thin frame. I went and supported her. After the sobbing subsided, she called me by my pet-name and asked humbly, 'Will you take me out? To see a film? A real film? To a restaurant?' When I nodded, she broke down again.

Shortly after the death of my uncle, my father began his battle with pain and disability. He had formidable reserves of willpower, and started off in fine fettle, mentally, even after a lifetime of fights with my mother, no mean antagonist herself. I inherited my music from her. My father and his brothers, my uncles, had no music. They were essentially modern bandits who sailed close to the boundaries of the law, crossing lines pretty often, and looked down on the arts, brazenly flaunting their own lack of culture as machismo.

My mother and her brother, 'my other uncle' as I called him, were, on the other hand, continually playing with music, the one humming extempore a few phrases which had to be continued or concluded by the other. Their own gifts made them look upon composition of music as a normal human faculty like sight or hearing and had I been born tone deaf I am sure they would have pitied me as a cripple of the worst sort or a monster and killed me by their indifference. My other uncle didn't marry, and there was no love between my parents, only lust, which, however, was intense and special enough to keep them faithful to one another. So, brother and sister expended all their love on me, but I understood my good fortune to be conditional on making good music, and early on I learnt the business of telling only a little of the music which arose in my mind, keeping most of it on store for the arid days when the muse deserted me. You see, the muse visited me sparingly but I wanted their love all the time. Both died shortly after my uncle.

My father lived for years after my mother died, till, like his brother, he fell, finally, a prey to their heredity of galloping rheumatism, which he had been fighting for long, and became confined to the chair. Love had never been lost between the two of us. My father believed in the essential wickedness of all children and felt no compunction in beating out vices from my system. We seldom spoke to one another after I left my father's house, and now, years afterwards, he had to shuttle between chair, bed and bathroom in my house. I was sure that part of the black depression which engulfed him arose from this helpless dependence on me. He had always derided my passion for music as an effeminate escape and now it was money from that music which paid for his upkeep. When he reached the stage of incontinence he fell silent. Left to himself he would not have eaten at all, but unlike his brother he was quite docile with care givers who had little trouble feeding him. Nights were sleepless and he started dozing off after lunchtime.

Slowly feeling crept back in my mind as I saw the motionless form, day after day, awake but with eyes tightly shut against the world, soiling bedclothes, waiting in indignity for someone else to wipe him clean and change his bag. The feeling was mainly one of forgiveness, extending to a sort of pity, but it did not exclude a repugnance for the elemental cycle of calorie and protein intake, digestion and waste production which seemed to be the essential and final residue of the human condition. Sometimes tears flowed down his face, and still I couldn't summon sufficient empathy to touch him. Of course, he would not have felt the touch, his mind was light years away.

All these thoughts and memories flitted cloud-like across my mind as I crossed the road to the general store, and lifted the horizontal desktop separator to enter the shop. Any change in elevation engaged the knees and stepping from the road on to the kerb was sufficient to send a streak of pain through the joint which was bearing more of my weight at that moment.

'Don't be depressed,' advised my friend the surgeon, 'Depression increases all pain.'

But, often, over the last few years, I had fallen into its clutches.

All the while, I was making a name for myself, spending banked assets from my memory. Very little was being added to my savings. Of course, I was doing important work. My musical training was of the traditionalist school which divided music into several sequences of tones and the performer had to keep to the tradition of rendering a composition which kept intact a particular tone sequence or, at most, followed a few allowed variations, and only the greats had been able to add one or two complete tone sequences which were new. But tone sequences fitted the times of the day, the seasons and emotions, and rendering a tone sequence usually implied a particular emotion in a particular season at a particular time of the day. For example, many great compositions had been rendered in the late afternoon about love fulfilled while it rained tumultuously outside.

However, I was equally attuned to the great symphonies where there was a sequence of different emotions, within a very general discipline of the chords, though even that was broken by the modern users of dissonance. I thought that there was more scope for originality in this kind of music. While I was wrung, bound and beaten into pulp by the maelstrom-like power of the great tone sequences, properly rendered, I wanted also to mix emotions and seasons, or make these follow in quick succession as and when necessary. I wanted to ride the maelstrom, and I originated an obvious method of synthesis immediately branded as heretical by the traditionalists. They were somehow kept at bay by my own teacher, who had been called heretical in his time, and now felt a fierce glee at having spawned a yet greater heretic than himself.

I did not, in fact, depart from the strict classical sequence. All I did was to take phrases from two or more tone sequences and juxtapose them, neither at random nor following any definite rule. How I did it I couldn't tell. My ear did it for me and I could feel that the result was a beauty and, at times, a grandeur which was overwhelming.

A critic wrote, 'His music took the world by storm.' The method began to be followed in real concerts and virtual music halls. His famous teacher always pointed to the undeniable beauty of his music, and when the traditionalists lamented that now every Tom, Dick and Harry would become a composer, he laughed in their faces and begged them to show them one who created a new beauty like his student did. But when he died, the heirs to his school promptly disowned his pupil. They had only envy for an originality and courage they didn't possess and were small men and women, the likes of whom have always in the history of art and music taken pleasure in denigrating greatness.

However, his popularity spanned the globe, young and old, the disciplined student of music and the uninitiated, and there was no reason for him to take the criticism to heart. To every one's surprise he slowly slid out of the world of music, and, in fact, became a recluse, in the popular sense—that is, he never met the media. After floating more and more fantastic surmises, the media finally let the world forget him. He, then, bought a little piece of land in the meadows at the foot of a hill, deep in the interior of a belt of forest, and raised a clay house with a tiled roof. But inside, all modern facilities were in place, for the sake of his wife, an urban socialite, who, her friends had warned him, was unlikely to last for more than three months. She proved everybody wrong and entered with gusto into the intricate social life of the original inhabitants of the region who had continually been pushed out of land reclaimed by them for agriculture. They had been pushed into the forest, and, then, out of the forest, as the forest began to be reserved increasingly for timber merchants alone, into small villages on the slopes of the hill. She organised childbirth, alternative medicine, handicrafts, cookery, knitting and needlework training during the years he waited for the music to start flowing again. His coffers were almost empty, and the little which was left he hungrily hoarded in secret.

She didn't understand music and her love for him was of the same protective and possessive nature as her love for her son, who grew up with the village children merrily, till her parents came on a visit and were aghast to find their daughter and grandson 'going native' as they complained on their return. They took him away and garaged him in a boarding school, from where he escaped twice by climbing trees which put down branches outside the school walls, and a compromise was reached whereby he read in the school as a day scholar while living in his grandparents' house, and spent weekends and holidays in the 'jungle', as his grandmother called the home of his parents.

The music maker dutifully tried to make music twice a day, but he was merely arranging and rearranging phrases which had already been expended by him, and nothing new came to him. It is this which decided him to stop public recitals. The only reason he could go on trying to make music in this house was what he thought to be the absence of an audience. He thought he was alone, here. But acoustic tricks caused the music to rise along the hill and reach the hamlets. The communities enjoyed his music, but were strong critics, too, shaking their heads if it didn't appeal to them, and doffing caps towards the little house if they thought a piece was really good. The music maker knew nothing of these listeners and critics. He only saw a shepherd boy who passed the window at which he liked to sit with his instruments, morning and evening. The boy stood for a while if he liked the music. Most days he walked his goats slowly past the window.

From his diary

At odd corners of the general store I thought I smelt her perfume. Of course, the brand was not too uncommon and many women wore it. Then, as I turned towards the desk I thought I saw her step out on the kerb. I abandoned my basket and limped out of the store. By the time I reached the kerb, no woman could be seen in any direction. Slowly I came back to the shop and completed my shopping. But the flood gates of memory had reopened. Feelings of sadness and ecstasy poured out to colour my mental canvas, usually a staid black and white, till it looked like a tropical rain forest together with all manner of exotic flora.

She was originally a student of his teacher. The teacher was, at the time, very short of breath. But he was a spendthrift and in no position to refuse students. So, he sent a student or two to the music maker, knowing he wouldn't dream of encroaching into his master's fees, while carrying out the task to the best of his ability.

From day one she tried to wreck the formality of the traditional relation between instructor and pupil. After first lessons at her house in the afternoon, she detained him, ostensibly to meet her parents, a chore which was soon over, the father proving as uninterested in him as he was in the individual in question and the mother casting a speculative look at him, to assess, as he understood immediately, sexual potential, and surprised, no doubt, to find a high score, gave him a second glance, but that was all. The real aim of the daughter was to talk him into accompanying her to a place where there were teenagers and music and dancing. He was a good antagonist and said that he practised tone sequences in the late afternoon. After she tried admiration of his discipline, advocacy of routine tempered with flexibility, indifference, and ridicule, and failed, she took the unusual step of taking him and his instruments to the roof where he could do his practice. He was, of course, already stimulated by their exchanges, and the promise of distant hills and forests in the view from the roof, together with the riotous skyscape that evening affected him deeply. He started creating music, without inhibition and didn't know when he had began to perform in full earnest, oblivious even of her. He stopped when darkness fell. She sat motionless all the while and was silent even after the recital was over. She rose when he did and led him downstairs. When she asked him if he wanted tea or coffee, there were tears in her voice. He knew he had been very good and wanted to race home to recollect the phrases and sequences which had come to him, and, of which, stingy that he was, he had used only a few.

Of course, she took him to the teenagers' hang-out one evening. He had little practice dancing and his teacher would flay him alive if he took alcohol, although the old fox himself never went to a recital sober, because, he claimed, that was the only way he could endure the music-less moneybags who frequented and, in fact, paid for public recitals. So, that was why he sat at a table nursing a glass of fruit juice and let the music flow around him. It was music from films, the standard stuff of music shows, but his teacher disliked snobbery and had taught him to find strengths to emulate in all forms of music, birdsong, the shepherd boy's flute, the boatman's song of the ebbing tide, the mendicant's songs of the mysteries of body and mind, the homesick blues of working men and women far from their native village, harvest songs, and the easy lilts of the music hall with their one-dimensional views of love and death, joy and sorrow.

She danced with two or three men one of whom seemed quite intimate with her, if dancing in a near embrace was considered an indicator. They danced cheek to cheek with fused bodies. Her face was positioned to look behind her partner, and she looked without break into the eyes of the music maker, and her lips moved, making promises, he understood, not to her partner, but to him. He was elated and fell into her spell, and so missed the most important conclusion to be drawn from the incident, a conclusion which could have saved him many sleepless nights, heartache, and stretches of depression.

Actually she also fell into his spell, and soon they became lovers. It happened on the roof below a sunlit sky and dazzling white mountains of clouds. The throaty sound of her fulfillment merged into the faint keening of a hawk on high, she wept and a great music arose in his mind around the theme. His hands trembled as he dressed, for the music became a pain clutching his ribs which drove him home and only dissolved after he had written it down. She started worrying when he went away abruptly, and, after a sleepless night, ran to his lodgings, creating a sensation in that working people's district with her disarrayed hair and disheveled dress. He was lucky it was early in the morning. Still, his mates of the lodging saw her and couldn't tell whether he was an unusually lucky bloke or a tragically ill-fated one, 'just waiting for the sky to fall', as the mess manager put it. They themselves were in different stages of morning undress when she turned up and there was a flurry of great unease as bath towels were hastily pulled out to preserve decency. She was unfazed in her bedroom slippers even in the middle of so much body hair which could not be hidden, and shook uneasy hands impatient to return to insecure bath towels, as she wished everyone 'Good morning' in impeccable society accent.

She made him describe what happened to him as she sipped lukewarm tea prepared by his room-mate, but how could he even try to put in words what he couldn't begin to understand or control?

They became inseparable. A good-looking couple, he, a favourite student of a world renowned don of the music world, and she an heiress, who set trends in style and fashion, their pictures were seen often on the fashion pages. She, they both realised, would make a competent musician but not anything more, and while she viewed this as a sort of separation from him, a concept which caused her great pain, he diagnosed a talent in dancing and set her training with one of the foremost traditionalist teachers.

Three years passed like this. For him it was a period of fecund originality. Music was always assailing his mind and while he surrendered his being to the waves, he didn't stop thriftily storing the greater part for a 'dry' day. Little did he foresee a dry spell of decades, but so overwhelming was the quantity of music which came to him then that he was able to last out his store even for so long a time.

She wanted to marry him badly at first, but he found his teacher was less than enthusiastic about such a project. He gave no reasons. What he said was this: 'The times have gone when the teacher governed all aspects of even the mature student's life. You can marry whom you like whenever you like and my doors will always be open for you. But ask yourself these questions that you are putting before me, and when you receive unequivocal answers, proceed on your journey.'

He didn't really obey his teacher. He caught the general drift of the teacher's opinion and decided that had the teacher been enthusiastic about the marriage he would have said so, and his ellipticities implied caution, and, at least, delay.

After three years, the inconsistencies began. In the beginning she had demanded all his time, and the tears filled her large eyes if he said he had work to do in the evening. 'Especially,' she said, 'don't take a streetcar and leave me on the street in the evening, I cannot take sunsets alone.' But, now, for example, on Saturdays she tried to meet him early in the afternoon, so that, before evening enveloped the city, she could say, 'Now go home and rest'. He made a test case one Saturday evening by pleading loneliness, but her response was to allow him to accompany her to her dressmaker's cottage, at which point he had to leave her. If they went to a show which lasted any length of time she would always be restless as if her mind was somewhere far away. If he stayed late at her home, she would be fidgety and rush to the telephone to make a call the the moment he visited the washroom. She didn't want him while shopping, and unwillingly he noted that the actual time spent over the declared activities might easily have been less than the total time spent.

When any of these incidents occurred, he was upset, and she would notice it immediately, to say, 'What have I done now?' and pout and cajole to make him say something. He remained silent because one Saturday afternoon when they parted he did ask her whose call she had received and answered, with the result that she started to weep and say, 'There is no one, but no one. Why do you suspect me all the time?'

The incidents occurred less frequently after any such flare-up on his part, but on the whole things became worse. She had always prepared a private meal for him at her house on his birthday, but this time the day happened to be a Saturday and she came to his lodgings with pastry from a shop. For some obscure reason, she had been celebrating New Year's Day so long by giving him a pair of cuff-links, and three pairs decorated the shelf which housed his shaving mirror. This year she forgot all about the cuff-links till she saw him wearing a pair he had bought himself. Of course, she wept.

He could not put his hands on any definite proof but his mind was ravaged by the inconsistencies in her statements and behaviour. She would neither admit the presence of anyone else nor could she seem able to give up the actions which so disturbed him. On the other hand, when she gave him time she filled it with a joy he never knew away from her, and their lovemaking was much more intense than before. His creativity reached new peaks when music seized him, though the quiescent periods, too, lengthened. But some habits were being etched in his consciousness which he didn't like. Whenever she said something about herself, involuntarily his mind went on weighing possibilities for and against its veracity. Not only was this compulsive calculation of time schedules and scrutiny of nuances of conversation occupying mental space and filling up time, he was being degraded in his own eyes. But he could neither tear himself away from her nor could he accept the inconsistencies without disturbance.

From his diary

Because of the pain, it took me longer that day to lug back the stores and provisions on the little wheelbarrow I had asked the carpenter to make, broadly on the principle of the luggage carrier. I was worried because never before had walking on level ground hurt me so much. I remembered the surgeon's frank confession when I asked him about the outcome of my bad knees. 'It is a degenerative disease, my friend,' he had said, 'and the rapidity of degeneration varies from one person to the next.'

I was tired, too, and dozed off on the first chair in the hallway on which I rested my body. The morning was over when I opened my eyes, and the shadows were just starting to lengthen. An impatience drove me to take a quick bath and peck at a cold lunch. I wanted desperately to make music. The first few sounds uplifted me. Quickly I soared into the realms of ecstatic joy and every time the high note was held and descent was about to begin, a higher note was reached. The music then began to span the happy webs, it was becoming a thanksgiving to her for letting me know what happiness was. The little puzzles were present as dissonances I couldn't drive away, but all littleness was banished to corners and swept out finally by the swelling flood. But she was beyond reach and beyond comprehension. The body of the music was joyous but, deep within, there remained the sorrow of intangibility.

When he ended, the shepherd boy rose. He had been crouching in front of the window all this time. He approached the music maker as he sat completely still, thoroughly exhausted and drained of all emotion, to offer a rare flower which bloomed only deep in the forest. He had searched out the bloom for someone else, but this the music maker couldn't know.

The music maker didn't know that the hill communities savoured the music he had made that day. 'The master has never made music as good and as joyous like this before.' But the women shook their heads. 'He gave a heart to the music, and the heart is sad.'

It was the age of communication with the speed of light, and his daughter was on the telephone by nightfall.

'The music company wants to contact you immediately,' she said after exchange of household news, which on his part included the state of his knees and the attendance logs of the hired help, and, on her part, the school grades of Elder, his older granddaughter, the commencement or remission of Younger's fever, the immunity of his younger granddaughter against the common viral cold taking a long time to develop, the travel status of his ambitious son-in-law, and her own troubles with the head of her redbrick university.

'Why did they want to contact me? Do they owe me money?'

She made impatient noises, 'No, no.'

He was on his hobby horse. 'Of course, they do. They have short-changed me all these years.'

'Father, listen.' Younger was bawling her head off, and her distraught mother called him Father, as was her wont when intensely irritated. 'They want your latest.'

'Toots, you know I am out of that world.'

'Well, for some reason they think you have done something out of this world also. Have you or have you not made new music?' She was still irritated, but Elder, it seemed, had succeeded in subduing her sister.

'Toots, I am always making music,' he allowed himself a hyperbole, 'But I have nothing for them.'

'All they want is a CD for evaluation. Today. You made it today. They must have a resident spy near your hut'. She was never short of money. So, it must be the personable and honey-tongued youngest shark of the four brothers who controlled the music company. She was approaching the dangerous age, he thought. Thc only hope was that sharks never succeed in concealing their teeth.

'Look, today, I made music for myself as I always do in the evening. It was not for the great uncultured.'

She was exasperated. That he knew from her use of 'hut' as a pejorative, a code-word for what she saw as his stinginess, ever since a wasp bit her one summer inside the house and the beginnings of a wasp's nest were discovered in one corner of a room. She had been quite hysteric, shouting, 'I might have died had I been allergic,' and cried loudly, rolling her eyes when he shrugged his shoulders to say reasonably, 'But you don't have an allergy to wasps.'

'They are not asking you for the crown jewels, no, no Younger, you're asking for trouble. Elder, Elder. The CD, Father.'

Younger must be kept out of serious trouble. It was time the conversation ended. He stated baldly, 'I didn't record it.'

'What? Not even on your Victorian recorder?'

'The Victorians didn't have a recorder.'

'Oh yes, they did. What about the phonograph?'

He thought he had diverted the flow of her thought. But, no, she rebounded back, 'You are really the limit, Father. Tell me clearly, is it on your recorder?'

'My recorder is out of commission for more than a month now.'

'Well, then, do it again.'

'What,' he knew she was no artist, a nuclear engineer by profession, an endangered species, too, in the greener vision of Gaia. But this was philistinism of the first water. 'What? What?'

'Re-create it.'

'Can you reproduce the quantum state before observation after you have observed it?'

For a full minute she was still with rage. Then, she replaced the receiver. But, thinking perhaps that he might die as her mother did before they could make up after one of their innumerable quarrels, she rang up again. 'Elder will go to your place tomorrow.'

This was good news. But he had to ask, 'Doesn't she have school?'

'Dad, dad, what is the date tomorrow?'

'Oh, oh.' She had shut him up effectively. It was the so-called Republic Day.

'Bye.' She was in better spirits after his faux pas.

In his younger days, he was highly focused on making a name for himself. Every bit of music he made, he made sure was credited to him. People, usually film people, were great thieves, and he took one such plagiarist through the courts till he was reduced literally to begging around the studios.

He began to question the reason for keeping a tight grip on life and fortune after his wife died. She was an intensely alive person and, during her illness, thought only of what she would do after discharge from the hospital. While the surgeon was putting in place the bypass channel around the artery which was worst affected by ischaemic blocking, she suffered a massive cerebral stroke and died instantly.

They had been great friends and generally refused to see one another's shortcomings, ganging up against the world in general and in particular against parents and children. He could not bear to go into her room and for months her dresses and cosmetic creams and lotions remained strewn over the bed, chairs, tables, dresser and bathroom shelves.

He constantly spoke to her as if she were alive. His children grew afraid his reason was going, and his son came to live with him. It was not a success, at least not from the stand-point of his children. His son retreated the day after he found his father and his wife engrossed in a three way conversation with his dead mother. He told his sister, who was expecting her first child, 'Toots, it is a madhouse. If I stay there another week you'll find mc taking Mamma to her favourite picnic spots.' He ran off, holding his head in his hands, when his sister's response was, 'Oh, how sweet of Papa. I wonder how many days my husband will remember me.'

What their father found was that apart from the crater-hole in his mind, everybody, including the children, slowly forgot the existence of this woman, her style of living, her modes of thought. It was as if she had never existed. He didn't really think that she existed now. He talked to her only to prove that she had once existed, and very much so. He was fighting the conspiracy of the world to rub her out.

For some time he thought that his work was all important, his work would not let him be forgotten. This only increased his insecurity because he knew well that he was cashing cheques on dwindling reserves. And, then, he thought of his teacher. In spite of memorial plaques and committees organising annual soirees in his name, who remembered the detailed rendition of tone sequences with little heretical twists of the tail, apart from one or two close pupils like himself? What might be remembered for a few years was the *name*. The man and his work had already been obliterated from collective memory, and their persistence in the minds of one or two individuals was of no account, and, in any case, would cease when they died.

He remembered his epics. In the form of a crane, the god of right living guarded a lake, and anyone who wanted water had, on pain of death, to give right answers to a set of questions. He remembered the question, 'What is perennially surprising?', to which the correct answer was, 'Every day some people are going to the abode of death. Yet, the rest of them don't really believe they will die.' What the god was saying was that nobody acted as if he or she believed that he would certainly die.

Slowly he attained a state of unconcern with many matters which had engaged his time and attention. He lost his nagging insecurity in the absence of new music. He taught himself the hard lesson of writing a piece of music deliberately, with phrases he had used in other contexts, and, while doing so, he discovered that thought could yield the key to constructing new phrases. Inspiration was fine when it was there, it gave you ninety-nine per cent of your music free, a birthday gift. But when it was not there, you had to work hard to make up for it. And, of course, it was never the real thing.

Instead of the smell of earth wet with the first showers of spring and the smell of the sea air split by bluish lightning, however faint, it carried the fresh from factory smell of the synthetic. Most people couldn't tell the difference and he again started selling music, some of which even invited rave reviews of the 'Maestro Returns' genre. But he felt like a cheat though actually he was working harder than ever before.

Finally, the wife of his teacher, a musician and critic in her own right, wrote him a personal letter. 'Artists and musicians have often to sell work which doesn't reflect the best in them to keep body and soul together. So far as I know you are not in that predicament. Why are you allowing the craftsman in you to camouflage as an artist? Have patience, music will come. I have seen such desertion in the case of your master, too. And what a return when it did come back. He almost killed me.' She actually used a coarseness which shone like a jewel.

He smiled to himself in the mirror and cancelled all deals. Most companies just issued 'Stop payment' orders to their banks, and remained silent, because they had seen many careers do the whirligig. But the man he had once ruined now had a music company of his own, and he not only said unkind words, 'Having dried up, what can he do but break contracts', but, through legal process, managed to impound his house as he didn't defend the case. Other music makers, in a rare show of support, threatened to blacklist the company, upon which they hastily retreated. He remained equanimous all through these happenings, so that his children knew of them only through the newspapers and descended on him like avenging angels. He cut them short and fled from the city.

On previous escapes he had walked twenty kilometres in four hours, but his legs were not acting up at that time. Still, in ten hours, travelling by various forms of transport he neared his destination, a hamlet where lived an old friend from the bachelor's mess so disturbed one morning by a girl. He was a school teacher from choice and not compulsion. A rising scholar from an oppressed community, he would have been welcome at the high tables of the land, but he wished only to serve his people and had no illusions about calls from the king. They were invitations to join the servants in purple who ruled over the servants in loin cloths.

From his diary

The last lap was through a forest, the hamlet being almost at the centre. When I entered the forest it was still night. There was a full moon and the minerals in the sandy path shone like diamonds. An hour or so into the forest, I was suddenly surrounded by four boys and two girls, who seemed to have sprung up from beneath the ground, with guns of different vintages in their hands. I displayed all the classic signs of surrender and sat down. It was a welcome intermission in my travels, an hour being my limit for a single stretch. They didn't believe a word I said but I understood that they would be taking me to my old friend who, it seemed, had advanced another logical square and become a guerrilla leader of sorts. He was very glad to see me, congratulated me on getting rid of the two women who had wanted to run my life, and introduced me to his wife who happened to be one of my captors, a cause it seemed for endless giggles among the girls.

I insisted on getting my holiday, and, refusing hospitality at the camp, dumped myself on his mother who knew me well and was immensely pleased to be able to complain the whole day against her son. Nobody in the whole forest, it appeared, was ready to listen to any complaint against their leader, the old darling informed me with paradoxical pride. There was a party at nightfall in my honour. After consuming much more sour wine than was good for me I called for their instruments and made music for the girl-wife. It was dance music, a potpourri of all my experiences over the past hours. There was love, carnal and sublime, oppression, suffering and revolt. The young people danced till they fell asleep, some in couples. My friend took me on a round of the patrols, and, seeing I was almost sleep-walking, sent me back with a cadet.

I slept for three days and three nights, more or less. Then, my friend almost hauled me up to make one more half-hearted effort to enlist me in their cause, as he had been trying to do ever since he knew me.

'What is the worth of what you are doing? This making music for the rich?'

'Don't your people like my music?'

'But it is not essential.'

And our arguments went on forwards and backwards, till honour satisfied, he sent me to see a cock-fight with one of his neighbour's five sons.

It was horrible carnage, and was technically outlawed. The cocks had sharp knives tied to their feet and were trained to kill. My companion, although of tender years, enjoyed prestige as one of the most ruthless trainers, and many placed bets on his cock, who finally won. In the tournament he had killed three other cocks and was himself heavily wounded. We hastened back home as he had to be tended to.

I thought I would ask my friend what the worth of a cock-fight was, more than that of the music I made or less. But, when he looked inquiringly at me for my final answer, I only said, 'You know I am an incorrigibly anarchic individual and if we both live to see the revolution you will have to come and shoot me.' He thought I was flippant and went off to check the patrols.

On his return, he woke up all sleepers. A patrol had seen troop activity near one end of the forest, and they were to march immediately. 'It is safer for you to travel on alone and come out of the forest on the other side,' he told me. Smiling through the tears which filled his eyes, he said, 'Write more anarchic music.'

I had barely cleared the forest when troops saw me. Some of them told me later that they couldn't believe their eyes, a man walking nonchalantly out from the forest. The commander again didn't believe a word I said, and convinced that I was a guerrilla leader from the higher echelons sent me on to headquarters. This saved my body and soul, as the alternative would have been questioning, which would progressively have grown more and more hostile, leading on to torture and an 'encounter' killing, because I would have had told them the truth about my locus standi and the lack of my knowledge about the guerrillas, and so would never have been able to satisfy them.

Headquarters, however, admitted a slender chance that I might be telling the truth and contacted the state police. The fact that they knew me instantly impressed headquarters and they immediately sent a blacksmith to cut open my handcuff and chains, and a barber to shave me. Given half a chance he would have removed my magnificent head of hair and sold it at a good price, but I raised a storm and made preservation of my hair practically into an issue of civil liberties. My son and daughter arrived by evening, signed some papers, and took me off. The troops had been impressed by my music which had been flowing effortlessly since the guerrillas caught me, and came out to wave goodbye, all except a highly ranked intelligence officer who had interrogated me. My son claimed that this character told him, 'If it rested on me I would have clapped him in jail. There is no doubt that he is a sympathiser of the rebels, and would have joined them had he been less comfort loving'.

All along the journey home my children tried to scold me, but I was in good spirits and either made music or pretended to sleep. In the end they gave up.

However, the music stopped coming in equal proportion perhaps to the fading of the memories of his holiday, as he always thought of this interlude in his life, but he had won detachment even from the vagaries of his music, and, besides, the interlude proved the point of his teacher's wife, the music would return from time to time.

He wondered why the children were so perturbed at his doings, nobody held them responsible for him. At first, the whole thing was a mystery, but, in a few days, he understood that it arose from a basic insecurity. They sensed his growing unconcern about the world and were afraid that it would extend to them, as, of course, it did.

His sense of observing from an astronomical distance, without the affect colouring what he observed, increased in the months of his daughter's confinement, which she decided to spend in the clay house. When all was said and done, it was easy for other humans to get along with him, and his children at least knew that detachment had not clouded his other sense of what he had to do in any given situation. His son-in-law, in fact, depended more on his judgment than even his own, a situation which his daughter didn't like—she was naturally surprised that he didn't rely more on *her* judgment. What would have been decidedly spooky, had the young people been able to imagine such a mind-set, was his indifference to the outcome of his actions.

His friend the surgeon said this was symptomatic of the typical depressive personality of old age after the loss of one's spouse, especially in the presence of chronic illness. But, then, he was a conservative man who liked to fit everything into the type-cast pigeon-holes of his illustrated textbooks and social prejudices.

In this situation did Elder burst out of her mother's belly. From the first, she made clear her claims and designs on her grandpa. His daughter started going to her workplace after a month of rest and the whole day Elder stayed with him. She knew her mother as a soft, pleasant, milk-spouting presence in her bed at night and her father as a weekend visitor. The grandfather had to give the bottle to her, change nappies, give her the daily bath and respond to her chortling. Her first word was 'Ma', and it meant mother but was addressed, perhaps as a complaint, to her grandpa, who soon learnt to respond to 'Granda'. This is not to say that her parents neglected her. They attended to all her vaccine jabs and bore their share of night watching during viral fevers.

The upshot was that by the time Elder learnt to walk and talk she had pierced his defences, a fact he realised when she spent a week at her other grandparents' place with her parents. The house seemed empty and time seemed to hang heavy on his hands. Even making music was a chore and not a Napoleonesque task of keeping the powder dry. Elder started going to nursery school with him, and her parents, especially her mother, started to discipline her, complaining of spoiling by the grandfather. He carefully observed everyone's behaviour, including his own, and decided against his daughter's charge. He didn't believe in the coercion of children and had found that Elder responded well to reason, except in the matters of ice-cream and chocolate. On the other hand, the talk of her parents about discipline was motivated mainly by the need to win peace and quiet after work.

He tried to detach himself from Elder's upbringing, knowing that a child was pushed off-balance by contradictory signals regarding discipline and behaviour. It caused him pain, and he was surprised to find human relationships still capable of doing this to him. Finally his daughter started to strike Elder in anger. This was bad enough, but worse was her attempt to build a theory of reward and punishment based on what was nothing more profound than 'Spare the rod…blah, blah, blah'.

He gently nudged his son-in-law towards shifting into the apartment they had bought before Elder came on the scene. He didn't want a frank quarrel which would prevent Elder from seeing him whenever she wanted.

He was desolated, something which only Elder realised in her own way. She telephoned every night and spent weekends with him. His misery had for the first time in his life made him slatternly and Elder took on herself the task, much beyond her years, of inspecting his socks for ladders and holes, collars for black circles, underwear for tears, and refrigerator for stocks (after a judicious removal of cookies; she loved them and had heard the surgeon grandpa say that they were not good for her Granda).

Younger arrived, and Elder was, to his intense relief, released from the pincers of her mother's exclusive attention and impatience. Younger was a bawler, in any case, and demanded more time from her mother and fought her disciplining with decibels. The fight was still on and her mother was not emerging a clear winner.

From his diary

Elder arrived early in the morning, a short, plump ball of love and lightning. This being a holiday, I was exempt from playing the game of 'School' where Granda was the pupil and Elder the teacher. Granda was always being scolded for bad work or for forgetting books or exercise books, crayons and erasers. Some days he had to call his Mamma and teacher would complain to her. There were extremely bad days when Granda had to see the rector ma'am. I was sad to see how reading, writing and calculation ceased to be the decoding game of enjoyable mysteries and became Class Work and Home Work, and even something you might think would be as light as gossamer like colouring a picture became a formidably weighty task of keeping evenly within contours. From the nature and intensity of the game I understood what she and her friends were undergoing in class.

A year earlier the game had consisted of Granda being scolded by the teacher for incontinence in the classroom, a perennial fear of every school-going child. Technically there were ladies to clean up the body and the mess, if any. But the fact of incontinence was stigmatised, and little did grown ups know how the shame of having done poo-poo in class drove many children to refuse to go to school, and amassed secret clouds of black depression and thoughts of suicide in their minds. Every Elder didn't have the scope to practise catharsis on a handy Granda.

But this morning there was no school and no school game, and Elder sat beside me at the window and gave a sign to start making music right away. She sighed as the first few notes floated up and settled herself into a ball at my feet. She liked the music, the nearness, and the peace. But there was something more in today's music, a march with a core of wistfulness, and, when I ended I saw tears on her face for the first time since her mother brought her back from hospital, wrapped into a white cocoon. In fact, she was famous for not shedding tears.

She wiped away the tears quickly, looking at me again and again to understand whether I had seen them, and soon sprang up, ran up and down the stairs, and scolded me, 'Mamma asked me to change the mosquito net, but I couldn't bear looking at your bed sheets and they are in the wash basket together with the old net and the pillow cases'. She shook her head in exasperation. 'Now, pay attention, Granda. Remind the washerman uncle about the clothes in the basket, when he comes. Why you won't buy a washing machine Mamma can't imagine.' Then, it was time to go. Her father had come for her. She gave me a hug and went out to meet her father and as she finally turned for a last good bye I caught her expression in the camera. Her father gave a wave and they were away.

From the window one could see the short pathway to the house, and beyond it undulating green fields merging into the brush of the slowly rising hillside. When I bought this land, the old farmer who sold it to me asked why I was coming to this god-forsaken graveyard of hope and ambition. In reply I pointed to the hills, green almost three fourths of the way to the top. I have never forgotten his reply, 'City dweller, the hills look soft and green from this distance. Come close, you will find only thorny bushes.' He was talking of people, and at that time I took pride in the thought that I was almost immune on that score.

As I idled in the armchair I saw a familiar figure take down the catch of the wicket-gate and replace it. I had then made no mistake in the city. She had actually been to the shop where I thought I saw her. Her hair was all white and she had become plump to say the least, but the beauty of the bones was there, imperishable as long as the bones lived. She rang the bell and, when I opened the door, stared in wonder at my face, for age had not been kind to me. No doubt, she saw the lines and curves which so annoyed me every day whenever I looked into a mirror. She smiled and said, 'Well, then, aren't you going to give me a kiss for old time's sake?' And we fell into one another's arms.

She wouldn't let me get up from the window once she saw the predicament of my knees. She explored the ground floor, located the kitchen, put the kettle on and brought the tea things. I told her where a bottle of brandy was hidden. She put just a teaspoonful in each cup, saying, 'Let's not start too soon'. I understood it was not a short visit.

'Who are you hiding the bottle from? Surely not the domestic help?' Her antennae were out.

'Well, you saw the kitchen. Would you say a domestic help keeps the kind of order you saw there?' I wanted to tease her a little.

She didn't meet my eyes. 'Are you seeing anyone?'

'What about you?'

'Look at me. Think of my age,'

'That is no answer and no ground for one. You are still the source of light wherever you are.'

She brightened a little, but persisted, 'From the way you are shifting away from my question I assume you are seeing someone.'

'Look at me. Think of my age.'

'But you are you.'

'Well, someone is seeing me.'

She fell silent and her eyes darkened. I couldn't bear to see her light diminishing, and dropped the photograph of Elder I had taken in the morning into her lap. I felt the old catch in my throat as her eyes grew large and lustrous.

'Isn't she a heart stealer?', she said finally.

She insisted on preparing a hot lunch. The women I have known all thought of food as their emotions were roused. They wanted to feed me well, when food was quite the last thing I was thinking of. I must admit, however, that she had become a competent cook and a knowledgeable one, too. The omelette she made was sophisticated.

I fell asleep with my head in her lap. When I awoke she had hardly stirred. She had been preparing a speech, and she began, 'I had secrets...' I shut her up with my lips, and her solemn mood passed. She laughed and pushed me away. 'Go, wash your mouth,' she told me.

I made music in the evening, achieving a serenity I had never touched before. She listened wide-eyed, and, when I finished, said, 'You didn't even think once of recording. Truly you are now out of the reach of everyone. No one can hurt you now, as I did once. But aren't you lonely there?'

I looked into her eyes. Minutes passed, and then the shepherd boy was there, with two of the rare flowers in his hand. My daughter was right. There were spies everywhere. I suppose, I thought wryly, the whole hill community knows of her. Indeed, they did, and talked of nothing else that evening.

We walked hand in hand slowly along the pathways through the fields without exchanging information which had accumulated over the years. It seemed there was an eternity to do this. It was a moonless night and, when dew started to form, we returned to the light kept at the window. While I washed after a light supper, she prepared beds in the two connecting bedrooms on the first floor. She came and sat on my bed, attired in my clothes. She hadn't touched anything belonging to my wife. I was trembling with desire for her. She put off the light and came to me. She wanted me, I could feel this, but she was not ready. She whispered to me, 'Darling, I am an old woman. Bear with me'. And when I comforted her and kissed away her tears she dozed off with her head on my arm. I stared into the dark sky. My heart was quite full.

Pins and needles in my arm brought me back to the ground. She stirred against me, at first softly and then with urgency. But my readiness had subsided and she woke up to look at me on one elbow. 'I am an old man', I said, and we burst out laughing at our predicament. We fell into a deep sleep and the night passed. Both awoke almost at the same time at first bird call and we were ready for each other this time. She wept all the time it happened as she had the folly to do forty years ago. When I finally awoke at first light, I was alone. So sure was I of her departure that I didn't start looking for her. On my desk downstairs there was a note, 'Perhaps I may even return'.

I sat at the window like a shadow, for an hour at least and then the music broke. Wave after wave, it swept me off, buffeted me and left me whimpering and trembling like a whipped child .

The note was soon lost, like all those of his papers which Elder didn't file. He searched everywhere for it, but it was gone. So, finally, apart from her evanescent perfume upstairs, there was no evidence that she had come. The shepherd boy only smiled when he asked him about her. Music, however, stayed with him.

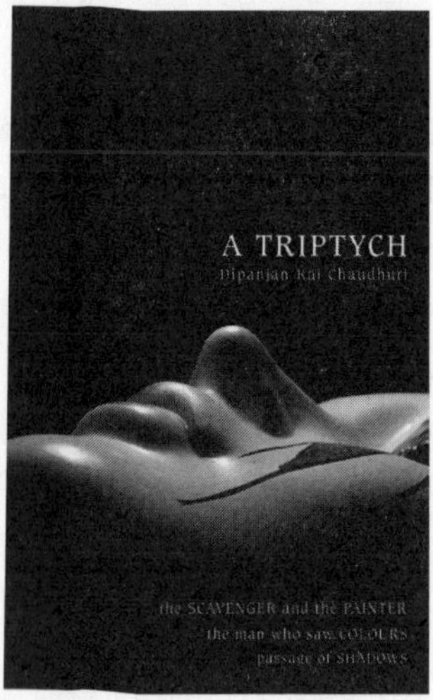

By the same Author: *A Triptych*

A *Triptych* presents three intense narratives set in distinctly diverse yet paradoxically convergent worlds, tailing the trajectory of some very unusual bonds: a scavenger, living off the street rejoices in his dark life, covertly watching from his post a desolate painter whose life is no more than a blank canvas. Their lives are connected by common fascination for the unknown, and there are startling secrets waiting to be unmasked ...; a young, city-bred girl on a visit to her native village to finalise the sale of common ancestral property is drawn to a neglected 'statue' staring unblinkingly at the horizon, perhaps astigmatic like Van Gogh, perhaps an atist and a philosopher slowly defining his vision ...; a little boy from a sleepy hamlet with a disturbing past and an insignificant present discovers an unusual and enigmati visitor, who he 'adopts' as his own, courting some unforgettable experiences that distill haunting memories for a lifetime ...

What makes this collection of three novellas a triptych is the intriguing carry over, from one narrative to another, of an intense mystery that not only negotiates unexpected twists, but defies the reader's imagination, each time, with its atypical denouement.

About the Author

Dipanjan Rai Chaudhuri, born in Kolkata in 1944, studied Physics at Presidency College in the turbulent late sixties and early seventies. Physics and the fight for democratic rights alternated as dominants in his life, with literature emerging from the background after his retirement as a don at Presidency, and a quest for improvement in teaching methods, especially in science and mathematics.

He has two slim volumes of poetry in Bangla to his credit, an influential tract on education, a publicist's diary called *Sovereign are the People*' along with a number of research papers in Physics printed in the foremost peer-reviewed international journals. Before the current offering of three novellas had come another such triplet called *A Triptych*.

Dipanjan Rai Chaudhuri lives in Kolkata with his wife. They have a son and a daughter and three grandchildren. As pains and aches start constricting his activities he puts more time into his project of a contemporary Bangla novel in three parts, the first of which has recently been published.